"Kiss me."

A sound of pure pleasure escaped from Tessa's throat as Griffin's tongue met hers. His lips were firm and he knew how to take charge.

He slid both hands around her waist, then stroked down over her derriere. "I thought we decided this wasn't a good idea," he whispered.

"You may have decided. I like it."

He pulled up her tank top and tugged it over her head. "You're a visual feast. It's been a long time."

Tessa took a deep breath, forcing her nipple into his mouth, each caress of his tongue sending pleasure careening through her. "So how long has it been?"

His chest shook as he chuckled. "So long I think they reissued my virgin card."

"Ooh. I've always wanted to have sex with a virgin."

"Then this is your lucky day."

Dear Reader,

Back in the nineties, devotees of *The X-Files* (of which I was one) would go around saying things like "Trust No One" and "Plausible Deniability" and "The Truth Is Out There." But the one I liked was on the poster behind Agent Mulder's desk: I Want To Believe.

So what happens when a man who trusts no one meets a woman who makes him want to believe? Tessa Nichols is a sensitive, a woman who can sense things that others can't, who has access to information that others do not. Her first job is to make Griffin Knox believe in her gift—and then she finds herself wanting to make him believe in her, and finally in himself.

A classmate of mine from grad school, Nancy Myer, is a bona fide psychic detective who has helped police departments solve hundreds of cases. Her stories fascinated me, as did her book *Silent Witness*. This fascination led to the creation of Tessa's character, back in July 2004, in Blaze #144, *His Hot Number*. I'm so glad that I now have the chance to tell Tessa's story!

For a sneak peek at my next Harlequin Blaze adventure, visit www.shannonhollis.com.

Warmly,

Shannon Hollis

Books by Shannon Hollis

HARLEQUIN BLAZE

SEX & SENSIBILITY
Shannon Hollis

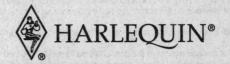

TORONTO • NEW YORK • LONDON
AMSTERDAM • PARIS • SYDNEY • HAMBURG
STOCKHOLM • ATHENS • TOKYO • MILAN • MADRID
PRAGUE • WARSAW • BUDAPEST • AUCKLAND

To Jenny Andersen, with thanks for the Denny's receipt

Acknowledgments

Thanks to Lieutenant Patrick Picciarelli, NYPD Ret.,
for his unstinting willingness to help my fictional
investigators do their jobs. Thanks also to Diana Duncan
and Jamie Sobrato for lending me such a snappy title.

ISBN 0-373-79207-7

SEX & SENSIBILITY

1

WITH A CRACK LIKE A GUNSHOT, the coffeepot broke and showered hot coffee all over his hand, the counter, and his pants. Griffin Knox wasn't the kind of guy to believe in signs and omens, but holding the black plastic handle in midair over his still-empty mug, he hoped this wasn't an indication of how the day was going to go.

In a moment he found out.

The cell phone he wore exclusively for communication between himself and his employer went *fleedeep* at five past nine. *Fleedeep* meant the summons was in walkie-talkie mode, which meant Jay Singleton couldn't wait the thirty seconds it would take to press seven digits and let it ring.

Singleton used walkie-talkie mode a lot.

Wiping the coffee from his hand and his jeans with a paper towel, Griffin grabbed the unit from the counter before it got drowned and pressed the respond button. "Knox."

"I need you at the house right away."

"The house?" As Singleton's vice president of security, Griffin's job was to make sure nobody messed with the vast tract of redwood, meadow, and low-slung architecture known as the campus of Ocean Technology in Santa Rita, California. If someone got laid off and came back waving a rifle, Singleton called him. If intellectual property slid past a nondisclosure agreement and into a competitor's lab, Singleton called him. If a visiting supplier from Singapore needed an escort, Singleton called him.

But typically his marching orders took him to Singleton's spacious office on campus, with its mile-high windows and en suite bath, not to the Carmel mansion perched above a crescent of beach like a coy starlet afraid to get her toes wet.

"I'll be there in thirty minutes," he told his boss.

"Make it twenty and I'll pay for the speeding ticket."

"Done."

Griffin gave up on the coffee altogether and put the pieces of the broken carafe in the trash can under the sink. There was no time to change out of his stained clothes. He grabbed his leather jacket off the back of the couch and slammed the door of the postwar stucco house behind him. The house wasn't much—two bedrooms, a bath, and a banana tree on the south side that stayed alive in spite of him—but it was his. In a life that, in one of those curious one-eighties he could never quite figure out, now belonged pretty much to Jay Singleton, that was a lot.

Griffin pushed his thirty-year-old pickup to the top end of high gear and kept a wary eye out for the California Highway Patrol as he sped down Highway 1. Ocean Tech might be based in Santa Rita, a town known for keeping the flame of the Summer of Love alive as every new class graduated from the nearby UC campus, but its CEO hobnobbed with the rich and famous on the greens at Pebble Beach when he wasn't inviting them to dinner at his home in Carmel. Griffin often wondered when Jay had time to run his shop, but apparently the wonders of mobile communications and an executive assistant who was a combination of Xena the Warrior Princess and C-3PO enabled Singleton to function as well in Carmel as he did in his office or anywhere he happened to be in the world.

Precisely twenty minutes later, the truck rumbled to a stop at the gate.

"Morning, boss," said the speaker under the camera that swiveled to look at him. A second camera mounted on an angle behind the vehicle took a picture of his license plate.

"Morning, Ramon." On paper, Ramon's title was Director of Private Security. In reality, he was the techno-wizard responsible for the safety of Singleton's property and everyone on it. Cameras were his specialty. "What's going on?"

"We got problems, all right."

"No shit. Details, man."

"The little *princesa* is missing. The *señora* went to her cottage this morning and found her gone. All of us got called in to search the grounds but there was not a sign."

"Sign of what?" He wished he'd had at least a cup of that coffee before the carafe had blown up. "She's just got her thong in a twist again about having to go to college. She could be shopping or walking the beach in a snit or God knows what else."

"Don't know, boss. But *El Jefe* is in one hell of a state. He seems to think it's a kidnapping. I hope that jacket has Kevlar in it."

"What have you got on video?" Surely to God the expensive surveillance system would give them their money's worth in a case like this.

"Camera 12 has her leaving the kitchen door last night at 8:10, and Camera 15 picked her up entering the cottage at 8:13. But nothing after that. It doesn't make sense.

She'd have to be invisible to leave without one of them catching it."

"Or she went out the window and down to the beach."

"Or someone helped her out that way. Good luck."

The gate swung open and Griffin drove through, dread and denial mixing in his gut like a nuclear soup.

Christina Singleton kidnapped? The fact was, it was only too possible. Jay had about a gazillion enemies. Competitors had tried to take over Ocean Tech, but he'd always beaten them off, saying that as long as he was CEO he was going to run his own shop, not take a cheesy senior VP role while somebody based in Houston or New York made the decisions. He was loud, brash, and didn't pull any punches, which was why the media hated him and Griffin got along with him so well.

When Griffin found himself with a shot-up leg and the choice between being a desk jockey with Santa Rita P.D. or an unemployment statistic, Singleton had got wind of it somehow and remembered a night years before when Griffin had done him a good turn. Griffin had been a rookie then, fresh out of the academy, and the sight of a carload of drunk computer geeks trying to climb a tree with a '76 Pacer would have been funny if it weren't so pitiful. He'd charged the driver with driving under the influence and hauled the most sober one out and told him to do something with his brain besides knock it out on the windshield. That had been Singleton, in his early thirties but as socially inept as a teenager.

So, after the shooting that had brought both Griffin's marriage and his career to a screeching halt, Singleton had stepped in and offered him the job as head of security for his fledgling company. At that time, Ocean Tech had consisted of five cold cubicles rented on one end of a warehouse. No one, least of all Griffin, could have predicted what Ocean Tech—and Jay Singleton—would become. And at one hundred-K a year, payback was a bitch Griffin was happy to live with.

He let himself into the house and walked across the foyer to Singleton's office. Each of Jay's ex-wives had had a go at the interior decoration of the house, but none of them had been allowed to mess with that room, which still looked like one of the cubes in the warehouse. Piles of publications, specs, contracts, and who knew what else layered the desk like some geologic formation. A huge computer monitor and the latest in technology, backup arrays, and telecommunications took up the wall beside it. The rear wall held another mile of windows, and in front of these he saw Singleton, oblivious to the dramatic crash of breakers framed by the glass, pacing back and forth as though he were crushing sand fleas into the Turkish rug.

"Hey, chief," Griffin greeted him.

"Twenty-two minutes. What did you do, take a break to yak with Ramon?"

"He was briefing me."

"Yeah, well, when I say twenty minutes, I mean it. And I'll do the briefing."

"Tell me."

It only took a few minutes to fill in the details. Amanda Singleton, Jay's fourth wife and the second to hold the trophy position, had gone to Christina's cottage to check that they were still on for a weekend shopping expedition to San Francisco, a hundred miles to the north. The cottage was within shouting distance of the main house, separated from it by a wide flagstone patio and a wisteria arbor. When Christina hadn't answered the door, Mandy had gone in, thinking she'd overslept. She'd found the cottage empty, the bed neatly made, and none of Christina's things missing.

"Not even her purse?" Griffin asked.

"It was gone," Singleton acknowledged. "So were her favorite jeans and a black sweater. Basically, the clothes she had on yesterday."

"That pretty much cancels the running away theory. Had the maid made up the bed?"

Singleton shrugged. The activities of the staff were none of his concern, unless the coffee kept perpetually hot and fresh on the sideboard got cold. Griffin decided that if anyone knew anything, it would be Lucia Gomez, Ramon's girlfriend, who cleaned up after *la princesa* with a patience that in him would have worn through on the first day. Eighteen or not, Christina was still a teenager. What was she doing with her own cottage, anyway? He and his little brother had shared a bedroom for their entire childhood and counted themselves lucky they weren't sleeping in the back of the family station wagon. But then, Dad had been a salesman and not Jay Singleton, and when he'd died, he'd left his wife nothing but his name and a hole of debt so deep you could swan dive into it.

One of the sweetest side benefits of his salary had been paying off the mortgage that had been the cross on his mom's back since that day.

"I'll start with Mrs. Singleton and the maids," he said. "I need to get as much information as I can if I'm going to help the detectives when they get here." At the stony expression in Singleton's eyes, Griffin paused. "You called the sheriff to report this, right?"

Singleton's jaws made a sound that Griffin realized was the grinding of his perfectly capped teeth. "No. No cops. Just you. You'll find her and no one will be the wiser."

Griffin stared at him. "What are you talking about? Of course we call the cops. If this is a kidnapping, it'll mean the FBI as well."

Singleton shook his head, negating every word. "If the cops get ahold of this information, it will be on the noon broadcast, with details at six o'clock. I know for a fact Barbara watches the West Coast news feeds and if she sees it, she'll yank Christina back to Boston so fast my head will spin. I had a devil of a time convincing her I'd get that kid to choose a college out here if she let her live with me. As soon as we find her, Christina's going to quit messing around and enroll somewhere and that's that."

There was no point in educating Jay about how careful the P.D. would be with a young woman's life in danger. Once he made up his mind, he was as immovable as a rock. "Have you heard from anyone? Has there been a demand for ransom?"

"Not yet, but she only came up missing an hour ago. It's just a matter of time."

"Stay by the phone and call me the second you hear from anyone. Set all the answering machines in the house to 'record' so at least we get them on tape. There might be some background noise to identify where they are." And he'd have something to hand to the sheriff as soon as he could reason with Jay. Meantime, there were things he could do. "I'm going to talk to Lucia."

Singleton resumed his destruction of the carpet's pile and Griffin left the study, intending to head for the kitchen to start his search for the maid. But she was waiting for him in the echoing space Mandy called the foyer.

"Ramon said you would want to talk to me," she said softly.

"Ramon was right." Their voices bounced off the marble floor and the flying spiral curve of the staircase that led up to the second floor. He gestured to his right. "Let's go in here."

"Here" was what Mandy had labeled the drawing room, as if she were in some English mansion straight out of the murder mysteries she read by the bucketload. It was the room she'd started with in her campaign to erase traces of the previous Mrs. Singletons, and even Griffin had to admit that the California Craftsman furniture and warm earth tones of the drapes and carpet were good choices. They echoed the colors of the Navajo rug on the wall that cost at least as much as he did in a year. He liked this room better than the French Provincial dining room and the medieval monastery kitchen, which were Mandy's next targets.

"When was the last time you saw Christina, Lucia?" he asked when she settled on the extreme edge of one of the couch's burgundy leather cushions.

"Yesterday afternoon, *señor*." Lucia studied the carpet. "She had gone for a swim and I saw her at the pool, so I took the opportunity to vacuum the cottage."

"You didn't see her after that?"

"I believe she had dinner with the family at about eight o'clock, and after that I assume she went to her cottage to watch television or call a friend."

"So when you made the bed this morning, did you see any signs of a struggle? Anything dropped on the floor? Anything to indicate what might have happened?"

The crime scene was irretrievably lost now. Lucia would have made the bed, vacuumed the rug, closed any open windows, and generally cleaned away any reasonable hope of establishing a trail for Christina.

"Oh, no, *señor*."

He hadn't expected she would notice anything, but having that confirmed still made hope drain away. "There was nothing unusual?"

"Not that, *señor*. I meant that I did not make the bed this morning."

"But Mr. Singleton said the bed was made."

"If it was, *señor*, then it means the *señorita* did not go to bed at all. I have not yet been to the cottage to clean it. Only Señora Singleton has been there."

She hadn't slept at the cottage last night? Griffin wasn't sure that narrowed down the window of the time of the crime, though. Just the opposite.

"Thanks, Lucia. You've been a big help." Maybe he could still find a clue at the cottage if Mandy hadn't done anything dumb. "Do you know where the *señora* is?"

"Yes, *señor*. She is at the cottage, waiting for you. She said I was to bring you there as soon as you had finished with *El Jefe*."

Was it too much to hope that Mandy had read enough of those books to know not to disturb Christina's room? Could something, just one thing, go right today?

"Let's go," he said.

2

"SO BESIDES FLAKING OUT of working on your thesis, what are you up to?"

Cell phone to her ear, Tessa Nichols stuck out her tongue at her sister, even though she was half a peninsula away. She walked across her one-room apartment to the only window whose very distant view of the water consisted of a vertical strip of blue between two buildings. On a good day. On a bad day, the grad student housing on the campus on the southern fringes of San Francisco sat under a fuzzy, cold blanket of fog and you couldn't see your hand in front of you, much less the ocean and its illusion of freedom.

"How come I have to *do* something? Can't a day just be enjoyed? Besides, I threw the cards and they said not to take on any important projects today."

That wasn't why she had thrown them, or what they had said, but with Linn you had to work up to these things gradually.

"Tessa, they did not. And I hope you're well past the starting stage. Term began a month ago. You should have that paper researched and outlined by now."

"Okay, how about this for a topic? 'Mind Games: Deviant Behavior in our Public Schools.'"

"That has possibilities," Linn allowed. "I could help you with data."

"Or how about 'Paris and Nicole: Attention-Seeking on a Global Scale.'"

"Tessa. I thought you were serious."

"You're right. It would only be good for half a dozen pages, and then what would be left to talk about? Hey, how about this: 'My Way: The Police Mindset in Today's Inner Cities.'"

"Don't even start with me," Linn warned. "You're not still burned about that street fair mistake, are you?"

"Who, me?" Why would she be burned about the most humiliating event of her life? "No, I'm thinking of changing my major from psychology to something else." Tessa grinned at the faraway strip of water and held the phone away from her ear half an inch, waiting for the explosion.

"Tessa Nichols! You will not waste another two years of your life. You're almost twenty-seven. I've been in two police departments and taken three promotions in the time you've wasted on social work, environmental science, psychology, and—and—"

"Literature," Tessa supplied helpfully. "But that was only for one term."

Linn—soon to be Mrs. Kellan Black ("But I'm keeping my name for professional purposes, thank you.") and showing the stress of every bride-to-be, no matter how anally well-organized—made an inarticulate sound, something like "urrrghh!"

Tessa took pity on her. "Sweetie, don't you think you should go shoot something? You sound stressed."

"I already spent the morning at the range," Linn snapped. "But it didn't help that the florist who is supposed to do our bouquets went into receivership this week. When I went to take some color swatches down there, there was a big Closed Indefinitely sign on the window."

"Color swatches?"

"Yes. From your dresses."

"I thought this was supposed to be a small wedding. Family and close friends. A dozen people, tops. How do color swatches fit in?"

"Have you ever tried to define *small* to an Irish-Italian family?" Linn asked with a sigh. "Whose only little boy is getting married? There are twenty-one—count 'em, twenty-one—people in Kellan's immediate family alone. The wedding party now includes you, his two sisters, and his niece Anna."

"Uh-oh. A flower girl? This is getting serious."

"Cooper, Danny, and Slim are standing up with him," Linn went on, naming the members of the narcotics team her fiancé had led at the California Law Enforcement Unit before he had been promoted last summer, "and his neph-ew, Seth, is ring bearer."

"Oh, surely not," Tessa teased.

"Yes," Linn said in tones of complete gloom. "I have entered the wedding twilight zone. Just call me Madonna and bring on the helicopters."

"Cheer up," Tessa coaxed. "Only eight more weeks and you can jet off to Mazatlan—"

"St. Vincent."

"—and forget about everything except spending ten days in bed with Kellan."

"That is the good part," her sister allowed. "I wonder if I can move our flight up a day and you guys can enjoy the wedding without us?"

"Don't even think about it. If I have to lace myself in-to that satin corset thingy, you have to show up to ap-preciate it. Why can't I just wear one of the dresses I already have?"

"Because your idea of pretty is eighty years old with its hem hanging down and one sleeve missing."

"Want to hear what I found today?"

"Not another ugly dress from grandma's closet," Linn moaned. "You should be putting that money toward paying bills."

Tessa decided to overlook Linn's opinion of her wardrobe. "I went to that great place on Post and found this fabulous cashmere sweatshirt for five bucks. Can you believe it? Obviously whoever priced it had no idea what it was made of."

"How can a sweatshirt be made of cashmere? That's a total contradiction in terms."

"I don't know. It's cut like a sweatshirt and has the bound neckline and sleeves, and it's nice and baggy, the way I like them, and it's this be*yoo*tiful ice-blue that actually makes me look human instead of like I just saw a ghost."

"You look human all the time. Your coloring is just subtle."

"Right. I look like a photographer's negative."

"Oh, come on. Marilyn Monroe had hair that color and look what happened to her."

"Um, she had a breakdown and took too many pills one night?"

"No! She was famous and sexy and drove men mad."

"I don't want to drive anyone mad. When it's time for me to meet someone, the cards will tell me."

"I am going to hang up on you now."

Tessa knew Linn hated it when she let the cards direct her decisions. In Linn's view, a sensible woman set her course and focused on her goal like a panther moving in for the kill. Tessa had never been called sensible. She was like her parents—creative and free-spirited. Well, maybe she wasn't quite up to living in a motor home and zooming around the country to art shows, but they all shared the same carpe diem attitude toward life. Except for Linn. She had always been the anomaly in the family—the white sheep, as it were. Linn needed schedules and to-do lists and procedure manuals. Tessa preferred to see what fate had in store for her a little at a time. And so far fate was holding out on her as far as men went.

It wasn't that she never dated. Men were yummy and fun and a good time. But good times were like tortilla chips—great for the short term, but after a while you wanted some guacamole and a few fajitas. Something substantial. Maybe that was the problem. Maybe guys couldn't handle a woman who wanted the guacamole on the tostada of life. Maybe it was the way she came across—Carson Takagawa, for instance, had told her that her sense of freedom was what had drawn him to her. Unfortunately, his sense of freedom was the kind that involved airplane flights and long-distance calls, which wasn't very satisfying in the long run.

She'd sure learned a lot about Japanese erotic art, though, which had come in handy since. Yes, she had a healthy sense of freedom—or to put it bluntly, she liked sex. She liked men's bodies—the firm heat of skin under her hands and the way they got so visibly aroused. She liked the build of anticipation when she knew a man's attraction was mutual but he hadn't said anything yet. And most of all, she liked the way a man and a woman could lose their grip on reality with orgasm. It hadn't happened often, but boy, the guy who could make her do that had serious keeper possibilities.

"Don't you dare hang up." She hadn't even got close to

what she wanted to tell her sister, but Linn's mind was back on the wedding.

"Kellan says he's going to make sure there are at least a dozen eligible men with a taste for blondes there."

"Well, if he's including those scary whack jobs he works with, count me out. They're nice guys and all, but I draw the line at concealed weapons. There is no way I could ever fall for a cop."

Cops were *not* yummy and fun, whether they were friends of your sister or not. After twenty-six years of having Linn laugh at her gift and discount the advice of the cards, the last thing Tessa could do was hook up with a cop who would spend the next twenty-six doing exactly the same thing.

It wasn't as if she'd never been up close and personal with a cop, either. She had—as Linn liked to say—data to back up her opinions.

It had happened a little over a year ago. She'd been minding her own business at a street fair in Santa Rita. She'd decorated her booth with care and had already sent half a dozen chattering customers on their way with readings taken from clothes or a photo, or simply a throw of the cards.

Then all hell had broken loose. Cops had come out of the woodwork, rounding up the vendors as if they'd all been running drugs out of their booths. Psychics, crystal sellers, soap makers, herbalists—it didn't matter. Everybody had been hauled down to the police station. And *hauled* was the operative word.

Tessa still remembered the granite strength in Officer Griffin Knox's hands as he'd manhandled her, wriggling and protesting, into the police car. In his cool eyes she'd seen the possibility of sympathy for baby chicks and home-

less children, but not for grown women innocently trying
to pay their tuition. Twenty-four utterly humiliating hours
later, she'd been let go without so much as an apology, because of course there had been nothing to charge her with.
It had just been a matter of the local P.D. having to keep
up their stats for the month, and peaceful folks of the tree-
hugging, New Age variety were easy targets.

She shook her head at the memory. "I mean never. No
cops. Not even to do the bridesmaids' dance with."

Her sister laughed. "Never say never, especially when
the maid of honor has to dance with the best man. Look,
I've got to go deal with this florist."

"No, wait." Tessa tried to push her unresolved resent-
ment into the little mental box in which she kept it. She
needed to spit out the reason for her call. "I saw something
and I need to ask you about it."

"What do you mean, *saw something?*" Linn's voice lost
its lightness. "Like a murder? A drug deal? Somebody
getting mugged? I've told you a hundred times you need
to move off campus and into a decent neighborh—"

"No, not like that. A vision."

There was a pause in which Tessa imagined all the
things Linn was trying not to say. "Tess, I really have to
go and deal with this flower problem."

"Please." Tessa hugged herself, wishing that, just once,
Linn didn't have to be cajoled into listening to her. Just
once, couldn't she say, "Tell me what you saw, Tess, and
I'll try to help"?

"I think someone's in trouble."

A sigh breathed down the line. "And you think this
because…?"

"After I went to the thrift store I stopped for a cup of
coffee, and someone had left their paper on the table. So

I looked at the entertainment section like I always do, and there was a picture in the society column of that software guy and his wife and daughter."

"Software guy. Okay, that narrows the field to about a million. We're next door to Silicon Valley, Tess."

"No, the big one. The guy in Santa Rita whose company puts on that Bay to Berries marathon you talked me into running two years ago. You know, the one where we started on the pier and wound up God knows where in the middle of a strawberry field."

"Oh," Linn said. "I came in twentieth in that race. It was fun. You mean Jay Singleton at Ocean Tech. What about him?"

"I think his daughter is in trouble."

"Again I ask, you think this because…"

"Because I was standing here this morning making a cup of tea and I had a vision of the same girl, the one in the photo with the Ocean Tech guy. She was tied up on a bed and there was a shadow looming over her. A man. And I had this feeling of anticipation mixed with fear, like she wasn't quite sure what he meant to do. That was how she felt, I mean. Personally, the scarf scenario is one of my favorites."

"You saw Jay Singleton's daughter. Tied to a bed. Tess, don't you think it's more likely she's on an estate in Carmel behind an electric fence with the most advanced technology in the known world to protect her?"

"I knew you wouldn't believe me."

"Even if it were this girl, how do you know she's in trouble? It could just be your neurons firing random pictures to your optic nerve. It could be something you saw in a movie once, and your brain put this girl's face on it."

"Like my brain has that much control over what I see.

I'm telling you, Linn, these visions I have are real. Just ask Connie Aguilar's mom."

Her sister the cop paused. "Finding that kid was luck and good guesswork and you know it."

"Finding her was the vision and *you* know it." Another silence. "Anyway," Tessa went on, "I think I should tell someone. You. The missing persons department. Someone."

"That you saw a random vision of a person who may or may not be Christina Singleton who may or may not be in a situation that might incite fear. No where, no when, no why. The officer on watch is going to need a little more to go on, Tess."

"Well, what would you suggest?" Tessa asked with her last reserve of patience.

"This is a hundred miles outside my jurisdiction. You can call the sheriff's department or even Santa Rita P.D., but I know their missing persons guy doubles in stolen property and has a caseload as high as my desk. Outside of ringing up Jay Singleton and asking if he's seen his daughter lately, I'd suggest—"

"What?"

"Getting to work on your thesis."

Tessa glanced at her laptop, humming softly on the counter, and with her free hand, brought up a window running the Internet. All companies had a page describing their executives and boards of directors. All companies had a "contact us" screen. Ocean Technology would be no different.

"Thanks, Linn. I'll do that."

"That is the first sensible thing I've heard you say all morning. Good luck deciding on a topic."

Tessa found what she was looking for before her sister had even hung up.

EVEN WHEN YOU KNEW what you had to do, it was best to check with the cards first. On the brick-and-board bookcase that divided the room and gave her bed the illusion of privacy sat the velvet bag containing her tarot deck, the front side embroidered with a picture of the Queen of Wands, her personal card. She sat cross-legged on her secondhand dhurrie rug, removed the cards from their nest, and laid them out in front of her.

Is that girl, Christina Singleton, in real danger? she asked the universe. Then she shuffled, cut the deck, selected three cards at random, laid them in a row and turned them over.

The Five of Wands in the situation position. Well, Wands meant drive or desire, and the Five symbolized struggle. So, something was pitting this girl against her peers or family. She wasn't very old, true, but something told Tessa it was more than the usual adolescent struggle for independence. This went deeper. She turned over the next card.

The Six of Cups in the self position. Okay, if the Cups meant nostalgia for the past and its simplicity contrasted with power in the present, what did the Six mean? Innocence. Optimism. The belief that things will be better in the future. Hmm. That last was pretty typical of a teenager, if her own feelings back then were anything to go by. Tessa turned over the last card.

The Ace of Coins in the challenges position. That meant the girl had begun something new—a project, a direction—with a view to the long term, like a seed planted with the hope of becoming a tree. This position was about turning adversity into accomplishment. So if the Coins represented some kind of talent or resource she had, then the

Ace meant the first step in growth toward her goal, an idea or plan she was carrying out with the long term in mind.

Tessa sat back, studying the cards. How did they play into her vision? That had been all darkness and fear and imprisonment, mixed with a kind of anticipation Tessa didn't understand. The cards said this girl had started something and planned to finish it, but the vision showed her to be powerless. How could that be? Were they both in the present, or was one a look at a possible future if things went badly?

In any case, her responsibility was clear. She got up and glanced at the computer screen to refresh her memory. Then she picked up the phone.

"Ocean Technology. How may I direct your call?"

"Jay Singleton's office, please."

"Community relations, technology, or personal?"

Tessa blinked. "Personal." The call rang through with no further comment. So Jay Singleton was embodied in three offices, was he? Kind of like God.

"President's office."

"Mr. Singleton, please."

"Press, calendar, or technology?"

Good grief. Why didn't they have a computerized answering system if all the humans could do was give her the verbal equivalent of a drop-down menu?

"This is a personal call."

Again she was rung through.

"Mr. Singleton's office," said a voice with such clarity and presence that Tessa immediately thought of some great stage actress, in her sixties but still elegant and able to throw a vowel to the third balcony.

"I'd like to speak to Mr. Singleton, please. It's a personal call."

"And your name?"

"Tessa Nichols. One *L*."

"Your company?"

Tessa hesitated. "I'm calling on my own behalf. It's—it's family related."

"Are you a member of his family?"

"No, but—"

"Mr. Singleton is working from home this week. I suggest you try him there."

"Could you give me his number?"

"Young lady, if the matter is family related I would assume you would already have his number. Since you do not, I can only assume this is a ploy to extract it from me. And that, I can assure you, will not work."

Yikes. What was she, Cerberus at the gates of hell?

"Could I leave a message for him, then?"

"Certainly." The woman's voice held satisfaction at having foiled yet another nosy reporter or impoverished inventor looking for a break. Then she switched Tessa into the voice-mail system, leaving her to talk to a computer after all.

Though she knew full well Cerberus would go into the mailbox when she was finished and hit the "delete" key, she said what she had to say. With a sigh, she hung up and leaned one hip on the counter, running her hands over the cashmere of her new/used sweatshirt, taking comfort in its soft embrace.

It would be so nice if, just once, somebody besides a computer would listen.

3

From the private journal of Jay Singleton

God knows how many hours Christina's been gone and no ransom note yet. This is destroying me. When we find the sonofabitch I'm going to take him apart, bone by bone. This is my daughter we're talking about here. Okay, so she hasn't exactly had the chance to see me as a dad. Ten years is a long time. But I was around in her formative years, wasn't I? Kids develop their personalities by five, and I was there then. It wasn't my fault that Barbara wouldn't let me have custody when we split up. It wasn't my fault I had a business to run and only twenty-four hours in the day. I was doing it for them, for chrissake, to put a nice roof over their heads and good food in their mouths. That was what she signed up for, right?

But Barbara is never happy. There's always something over the horizon that she has to have, and once she gets it, she's looking out the window again. I hope she didn't teach that to Christina. I hope the schmuck she married realizes it before she drains him of all his capital.

Christina asked to come to me. That's something, isn't it? It's only been four or five months and I think our relationship is pretty good. She seems to like Mandy, anyway. Except for Barbara, I'm a good judge of women. But then, without Barbara I wouldn't have Christina, so there you are. The sweet with the bitter.

God, I hope she's okay.

Why doesn't the bloody phone ring?

GRIFFIN STOOD in the middle of what he supposed would be a crime scene if he could find any evidence that there had been a crime. Something had happened to Christina between eight o'clock last night and eight this morning, and damned if he could find one thing that would tell him what it might be.

He glanced at Amanda Singleton, who had been with him since he'd begun work on the cottage four or five hours ago. Mandy was a blonde with bombshell curves and the kind of sleekness that came from hours at the gym and salon. Her hair had been skillfully and expensively cut to fall around her shoulders in artful disarray, and her aquamarine eyes were not the result of genetics but contact lenses. When he'd first met her he'd expected every stereotype in the book, but Mandy had soon set him straight on what happened to nice people who made stupid assumptions. She was honest, kind, and instead of being raised to the heights of wealth from the trailer park, she'd had her own legal career in Silicon Valley before she'd joined the corporate law team at Ocean Technology and been sucked into the orbit of Jay Singleton.

People often made the mistake of treating her as though she should be wearing tight jeans and big hair. They didn't make it twice.

"There has to be something else you can try." Mandy pulled on a bow-shaped lower lip. "The fingerprint kit turned up nothing but Christina, me, and Lucia. There are no footprints outside the windows and doors, not even

Christina's because God knows she wouldn't go near dirt even if she were forced. No ransom note, no goodbye note, no suicide note. Nothing missing but the clothes she had on and her purse. Not even a backpack." She released her lip and frowned at Griffin. "How could she vanish without a trace? Not to mention her makeup."

"To quote an old episode of *The X-Files,* nothing vanishes without a trace. There has to be something. We just haven't seen it yet."

"Okay, Mulder." Mandy gave up on the cottage and led the way outside to the little patio covered in wisteria vines where a person could drink their coffee and contemplate the multimillion-dollar view of the Pacific purling in below. "If you were going to just walk away in the middle of the night with your purse and the clothes on your back, what direction would you take?"

The breeze blew the scent of salt water and drying seaweed toward them. "The beach." Griffin turned to the north and gestured expansively toward the house. "Not the garage, since her car is still here. But what about the neighbors?" He made another quarter turn, toward the acres of scrub oak, wild grass, and fern that separated them from the nearest house.

"Overnight? Without a call to tell us she was there?"

Griffin had to admit this was unlikely. "I'll check them out anyway."

"I think the beach is the best bet." Mandy jumped down from the flagstones of the terraced patio to the lawn sloping away to the beach. "What if we see footprints? Maybe they can tell us something."

By this time of day there would be fifty sets of prints from day trippers and people walking their dogs on the beach, which had a public right of way. But they had nothing else to go on, and Griffin could use the walk to clear his head. Maybe if he came back in half an hour, he'd see something he'd missed.

They were nearly across the expanse of lawn, striped light and dark by the back-and-forth course of the gardener's lawn mower, when they heard a cry from the direction of the house.

"*Señora!* Señora Singleton, wait!"

Lucia leaped down the terrace steps and tore across the lawn after them, her hair falling out of its neat ponytail and the fabric of her white cotton shirt flapping against her.

Griffin headed for her at a run. "Lucia, what is it? Did the kidnapper phone? Is there a ransom demand?"

She clutched his arm, gasping, as Mandy pounded up to them. "Yes, *señor*. The kidnapper left a message at *El Jefe's* office not one hour ago."

WHEN THEY REACHED Singleton's office in the house, it was Griffin who was out of breath and Mandy who looked as if she'd just come in from a relaxing session at the tanning salon. Damn, he had to bump up his morning jog another mile.

"What have we got?" he demanded.

Singleton punched a button on his phone console. "This was in my personal voice mail at work."

"You have fifteen new messages—" a computerized female voice informed them sternly from the speakerphone. Singleton punched two keys. "Message twelve. Received today at 11:55 a.m."

Another female voice, younger and much more uncertain, spoke. "Mr. Singleton, my name is Tessa Nichols and you're an unbelievably difficult person to reach. I need to tell you something about your daughter. I believe she's in trouble. Please call me on my cell at 415-555-8076. Um, thanks. Bye."

Singleton poked at the console again and the automated voice grimly wished him a pleasant day. Then he looked up at Griffin. "I wouldn't have expected a woman."

"You think that's a kidnapper?" Griffin didn't. That voice hadn't been much older than Christina's, and a helluva lot less self-assured. On top of that, her name was setting off a bell. It was a name he knew, from somewhere in the dusty cabinet of case files in his head.

"What else?" Singleton demanded.

"Typically, kidnappers are more vocal about what they want," he said dryly. "Sounds to me like she's a witness who's seen something. We've got piss-all else to go on, so I recommend calling her back."

Instead of replying, Singleton used the speakerphone again and pressed the digits of the Nichols woman's number, and while it rang a breathless silence descended on the room.

"Hello, Mr. Singleton."

Griffin blinked, then recovered. Of course she knew who was calling; she obviously had caller ID. Then he frowned. He'd set up the house system with the phone company himself. They had every blocker known to man on the house line, so that no ID would show.

How had she done that?

"Tessa Nichols?" Singleton asked.

"Yes. Thank you for returning my call."

"What else was I going to do? But let me tell you right now, if this is some kind of blackmail scheme, it's not going to work."

The airwaves hissed for a moment. "Blackmail scheme?" the woman said blankly.

"What I'd like to know is how you got her off the estate so easily."

Griffin closed his eyes. Jay Singleton on a rolling boil was not easy to shut down.

"Mr. Singleton, she isn't with me."

"Okay, so you have an accomplice holding her. Spit it out. Tell me your demands and I'll tell you to go to hell. But hear me now, sister. If anything happens to my daughter I'll kill you and your accomplice with my own bare hands."

There was a second of silence. "Oh, my God, he *kidnapped* her. No wonder she's afraid."

"Who kidnapped her?" Griffin couldn't keep still another second. "What do you know about it?"

They heard her draw in a breath. "Is there someone there with you?"

"Of course," Singleton snapped. "Griffin Knox is my security guy. Former cop. So answer him. How are you involved?"

"I don't know anything about it except what I saw," the woman said in a noticeably cooler tone, and Griffin's gut went, *Aha. I knew it. A witness.*

"What did you see?" he asked.

"She was tied to a bed with scarves. Cotton ones, I think." Her voice picked up speed with the memory. "You know, those cheap bandannas you can get at any discount store. He was looming over her, but I couldn't see his face. And she was feeling anticipation mixed with fear mixed with something else, but I can't really describe it. She— she was naked. At least from the waist up."

"Where were they?" Griffin asked. A witness. A real witness, whose recall might be painful to listen to, but helpful nonetheless. For the first time, he began to hope they might get somewhere. That hope roiled in his gut along with the awful knowledge that someone had stripped Christina and was holding her captive for God knew what reason.

"I saw them in my vision," she said.

"Where's that? A club? A hotel?"

Another pause. "No. In a vision. Like, you know, a dream? While I was standing here in my kitchen, drinking tea. It was vivid and in color, the way they are when it's real, so I knew it wasn't just a random bunch of neurons affecting my optic nerve, like my sister says. In fact, I think—"

But they never heard what Tessa Nichols thought, because Griffin just remembered where he'd heard her name. He leaned over Singleton's desk and stabbed a button on the console. The light on the open line went out.

"If there's anything I can't stand," he said tightly into the silence, "it's a fraud."

TESSA HIT "dial last incoming number" on her cell phone, thinking they'd been cut off, but when no one answered she realized they'd hung up on her.

Why would no one listen when it was so important? A girl's life could be in danger, here. You'd think they'd want to track down every lead they had.

It was that man who'd done it. Tessa knew it as surely as she knew the fabric those bandannas had been made of. Singleton hadn't even told her who he was when she'd recognized the voice—that baritone almost-drawl that held hints of sagebrush and wide-open spaces, the kind of voice that could seduce or betray and still sound just as appealing.

Officer Griffin Knox.

Almost of its own volition, her hand crept up to massage her upper arm, where the bruises from his fingers had been. Because she hadn't gone into the police car willingly. She'd struggled and yelled and finally he'd grabbed her and shoved her in with an herbalist who was as angry and clueless as she was. And all the way downtown he'd lasered her in the rearview mirror with those vivid blue eyes in a face that shouldn't have worn such anger. Lines fanning out from his eyes told her he was a man suited to the outdoors—maybe even a man who laughed. He had the kind of mouth made for wooing a woman's body, with sculpted, mobile lips. Despite the bruises, she'd had to admit his hands held strength in long, capable fingers. And he was tall, too. She was a pretty respectable height and still the top of her head had only come to about lip level on him.

Quit thinking about his lips, you nitwit. The guy had arrested her and she'd bet ten bucks he'd been the one to hang up on her as soon as she mentioned the vision.

He was like Linn. If it couldn't be bagged and tagged, he wasn't interested in hearing about it. In fact, Linn was probably the only reason Tessa had been released that day. She'd called her from the booking area and Linn had dashed across the parking lot from the Santa Rita P.D. building to the county lockup to spring her before her name got into the system and messed up her job prospects for good.

Tessa had walked out of there feeling dirty and ruffled and thankful that there were sisters who, while they didn't believe in your gift, at least believed in your integrity. There was no way Tessa was dealing in petty fraud and Linn had wasted no time in setting Officer Knox straight on *that* score.

But there had been something in those eyes in the rearview mirror, some kind of pain that hadn't had anything to do with her…she'd just been in the way.

Tessa shook off the thought and went to pick up her cards. As she knelt on the ancient carpet, the phone rang.

Probably Linn, fussing about flowers. Didn't she remember that Kellan's mom had been a florist? Why didn't she dragoon her into helping?

No, wait. It was—

"Ms. Nichols, this is Jay Singleton."

Ooh, how about that. He wasn't using the speakerphone. She must be moving up in the world. "Didn't you hang up hard enough the first time?" she inquired, sounding every bit as polite as his robot of an assistant.

"I want to apologize. My security guy doesn't believe in visions and all that. I can't say I do, either, but we've got nothing else to go on."

"What exactly has happened, Mr. Singleton?"

He sighed, the sound of a powerful man rendered powerless and deeply unhappy about it. "I don't know. My daughter, Christina, went to her cottage around eight last night and that's the last anyone has seen of her. Nothing is missing but the clothes she was wearing and her purse. No one saw anything. We've had no demand for ransom. My wife and I are frantic."

"What do the police say?"

There was a beat of silence. "I haven't notified the police. I have reasons for wanting this investigation to be private."

Tessa wasn't the sister of a state investigator for nothing. "Mr. Singleton, whatever your reasons are, you have to put them aside and call in the cops. They have huge resources and systems set up to deal with just this kind of thing."

"No."

"But—"

"I'll explain why when you get here."

"When I—what?"

"Whatever your services cost, Ms. Nichols, I'll double it. You seem to have information no one else does. Despite what Griffin has been saying to me for the last fifteen minutes, I want you down here helping us. Whatever you have, these visions or dreams or whatever bullshit they are, I want you here where you can tell me about them. Then maybe we can gather some clues to go on."

Tessa's mouth had been hanging open since *double it.* She closed it on *bullshit.*

"Mr. Singleton, I can't just drop everything and drive a hundred miles to tell you about a vision if and when I get one. They're sporadic. Undependable. They come when they want to. This is not pay-per-view."

"Triple."

"What?"

"Whatever you charge, I'll triple it."

"My normal consultation fee is twenty dollars an hour, but I'm not going to—"

"Fine. Sixty. Starting now. And clock your mileage down here. Bill me by the day, and I don't care how many days it takes. Better come prepared for a week. I'll see you in—" she heard a rustle and imagined him shooting back his cuff to look at his Rolex "—two hours. Any longer than that and I'll send Knox up there to get you."

Now, *there* was a happy prospect.

Tessa glanced at the worktable, which was piled with books and references and good intentions. She thought about her thesis. And her student loan. And the bills, sitting in their own little pile on the Formica counter. Sixty dollars an hour times eight hours a day times seven days a week equaled—

Who cared what it equaled? Jay Singleton, one of the most powerful men in Silicon Valley, *believed* her. Her, Tessa Nichols, at whom her sister rolled her eyes even as she was springing her from jail. He believed her, and to her dried-up self-esteem it felt like rain falling in the desert, sweet and cool.

"That won't be necessary," she said. "See you in two hours."

4

From the private journal of Jay Singleton

She's coming.

Money talks, there's no way around it. Wall Street would laugh if they could see me now, but hey, everyone knows the stock market is half bluff and half juju anyway. Psychics probably use the art of probability with more skill than Alan Greenspan.

Bottom line is, I'm desperate. I have to do something, and if calling in a psychic is the only thing to do, that's what I'll do. Griffin will go ballistic, but it's not the first time. I can handle Griffin—or anyone else, for that matter.

The only one I can't seem to handle very well is Christina. It's a good thing this diary is private and I wrote my own code to create it. Even when I die, no one will be able to hack into it and see what I was thinking. But I was talking about Christina. I remember the day she was born. Thirty-six hours nearly killed Barbara, but even she agreed the baby was worth it. Red and scrunched and squalling and absolutely beautiful. I was afraid to hold her. She was wiggly and wet and so noisy I thought I'd split an eardrum. But I'll never forget it. I fell in love that day. Oh, I've loved women. I love Mandy, for God's sake. But not the way I fell for that baby. When she learned to walk and I'd get home at night, she'd come tottering toward me with both arms out…I'd fall to my knees, not to bring myself down to her level, but because they'd just gone weak with love.

Who's got my baby now? Is he hurting her?

No. Can't think about that. I'll go nuts if I do.

One hour and forty-five minutes to go. Come on, psychic. Get a move on.

"You did what?" Griffin stared at his employer, feeling as if his jaw had come unhinged.

"You heard me. I hired that Nichols woman."

"As what, for God's sake?"

Singleton shrugged and kept one eye on the flickering columns of stock market activity on his computer screen. "As resident psychic, consultant, whatever. Doesn't matter. If she has information, I want it, and I want it here, where I can access it twenty-four/seven."

Griffin bit back the urge to ask the man who paid his salary if he'd completely lost his mind.

"I didn't know you believed in that stuff," he said instead. Jay Singleton possessed the most ruthless intelligence Griffin had ever come across. Give him a piece of software and some financial projections and he could create a company out of nothing. But this?

"I don't have to believe in it," Singleton snapped. "I believe in results. She has more information than we do, so I want her here. I don't care how she gets it, I just want it available to me."

"She could be scamming you."

"So you said. But why call me out of the blue when no one but this household knows what happened? The timing is too neat for it to be anything but what she says it is."

"Someone in the house could have called her. They could be capitalizing on this, splitting whatever you're paying her."

Singleton shook his head. "Sixty bucks an hour isn't enough to make it worthwhile. No motive."

Griffin could think of a lot of people for whom sixty bucks an hour was plenty of motive. But his boss's mind was made up, and that was that. Not only was he going to have to do without the resources of the police department, Griffin was going to have to tolerate a con on his own turf—at least until he could prove it.

He hadn't been able to prove anything with Tessa Nichols last time, but this time he was going to succeed.

A CANDY-APPLE-RED 1966 Mustang convertible was made for one thing—well, okay, maybe two things. Tessa grinned at the curves of Highway 1 as the cliffs dropped away to her right and she let the car have its way with the road.

It had been a long time since she'd hit the highway and driven somewhere just for the sheer pleasure of it. Most of the time the Mustang sat in her parents' storage box while they flitted from state to state. It wasn't practical to own a car in the city—just the thought of parking on some of those hills was enough to make her shiver—but once in a while, on a brilliant late-summer day like today, a cruise down the coast was just what the doctor ordered.

As for the second thing…she'd just leave that one up to the universe.

At twenty minutes past the two-hour time designated by Jay Singleton—she couldn't help it if she'd run into unseasonable beach traffic in Santa Rita—she pulled up to a big, black gate and checked the address Singleton had given her.

Yep. This was the place.

"Ms. Nichols?" the gatepost asked politely.

She blinked at it. Plaster. Ivy. No mouth.

Then she saw the camera and the speaker box. "Yes," she said.

"We're expecting you," the voice said. "Please drive up to the house and someone will take your car to the garage." The voice paused. "Nice ride, by the way."

"Thanks." She grinned at the camera. "Call me Tessa."

"And I am Ramon."

"Guardian of the gates?"

"Keeper of the cameras."

"The eye in the ivy." Tessa loved a word game.

Something buzzed in the background, and an angry voice she couldn't make out said something that probably wasn't nice.

"Mr. Singleton is waiting for you," Ramon informed her in a tone considerably more subdued that it had been a moment ago.

"Thanks, Ramon. Talk to you later."

The ten-foot wrought-iron gates swung open and Tessa let out the clutch and drove through. The driveway wound through a wilderness of scrub oak and native grasses. A tiny brown rabbit the size of a man's fist hopped across the asphalt in front of her and she touched the brake gently. A covey of quail bobbed down the side of the drive and vanished into a bramble thicket shaded by fern. Tessa had to admit it wasn't often you found a rich guy with the sense to live with an environment instead of imposing himself on it with acres of green lawn that would suck up more water than most small towns.

It wasn't until she got to the house that she saw the terraced garden and the lawn that sloped away to the ocean.

Okay, so he couldn't quite resist the statement that the lawn made. But she gave him points for the rest of it.

The young man standing in the driveway tried to talk her into leaving the keys with him. "I'll park it," he promised her. "The garage is just over there, behind the trees."

"No can do." She smiled at him, but he was too nervous to smile back. "Nobody drives this thing but me or my dad. No offense. I'll park it and be right back."

"But Mr. Singleton—"

"Mr. Singleton can wait five minutes."

In a moment she discovered that Mr. Singleton could not.

She'd just parked the car in a garage that was so beautifully appointed with wood trim and a spotless, grease-free linoleum floor that she would have cheerfully signed a lease and moved in, when a man strode around the curve. In his late forties, he was dressed in gray wool trousers, and a knotted tie hung carelessly from the neck of a white dress shirt. His thick brown hair stood on end, as if he'd run agitated hands through it, and a brown beard fairly crackled with belligerence.

Jay Singleton. He looked much angrier than he had in the newspaper photo.

She slammed the car door shut and hefted her wheeled suitcase—used once prior to this, since she hadn't inherited her parents' urge to ramble—out of the backseat.

"What do you think you're doing?" he said in a voice pitched just on the near side of a yell. "Robin gets paid to park your car and take your bag in."

Tessa snapped the handle of the suitcase out to its full length and trundled past the convertible Jag and the two BMWs in the other spaces. "Well, as I explained to Robin, nobody drives this car but me and my dad. I'm perfectly capable of parking it. Nice garage. If you ever want to rent it out, call me first, okay?"

He stared at her as if she were insane, while she matched his long stride easily on the return journey up the driveway.

"And now that you've parked it, maybe you'd care to explain why you've kept me waiting for half an hour?"

Tessa glanced at the watch she'd put on because technically this was a paying gig and a person should make the effort to appear businesslike. "Oh, did I?"

The guy looked as if he was going to bust a gasket.

"If we're to have a successful partnership," he said with careful enunciation, "don't keep me waiting."

Tessa stopped at the bottom of the fan of stairs that formed the entrance to the Spanish style house. "Mr. Singleton, if you don't mind me saying so, you need some serious vitamin B therapy. Your stress levels must be off the charts."

"I do not need vitamin B therapy. What I need is my daughter back and for people I'm paying to do a job to show up and do it when I ask them to."

Did he always grind his teeth when he spoke? Up close and personal, she saw that his eyes were light brown, the color of a good, strong cup of tea.

Strong. Powerful. With the patience of a hypoglycemic crocodile.

"I want you to get your daughter back, too. As I explained on the phone, you can pay for the job but it's totally up to the universe whether I actually get a vision or not. It's not something I can control, and it certainly isn't going to produce results just because you want it to."

This, it appeared, was not the right answer.

"I understand about the—the unreliability of these visions." Muscles clenched in his jaw. "But I don't tolerate unreliability in my people."

Tessa shifted her stance, putting her weight on one foot and cocking her hip. "A, I am not unreliable, since I'm here when you requested I be here. And B, I am not one of your people. I'm offering you my abilities out of the goodness of my heart, but I can leave the same way I came. I don't operate according to your schedule, Mr. Singleton. I need to be in a safe, nurturing environment where all I have on my mind is opening myself up to finding your daughter. If you're going to rant and rave every time I open my mouth, this is not going to be a success. Do I make myself clear?"

Odds were good that no one had spoken to Jay Singleton in such a way since, gosh, maybe his fourth-grade teacher.

But hey, she was in the right. It was perfectly true that she needed to focus, and being yelled at every time she forgot his schedule was going to spoil that focus. Did the guy want to find his daughter or not?

She waited, her calm gaze on his infuriated one, until his mouth stopped working and he could speak.

"I am *this close* to firing you," he finally managed to say past clenched teeth, holding his thumb and forefinger a quarter of an inch apart.

"I see that," she said cheerfully. "But do me a favor and think about the vitamin B, okay?"

IF HE COULD JUST get through the next ten minutes, Griffin figured they could turn the girl over to Mandy to stick in a room somewhere and then he could get on with finding Christina. He heard raised voices out in the driveway but resisted the urge to step to the door to see what was going on. He wasn't going to dignify her presence here with that much attention.

The door to the office swung open and the girl walked in, Singleton right behind her.

She flinched, as if she felt the force of his animosity, and then her gaze swung to his and locked.

Her wide-set blue eyes were filled with a mix of defensiveness, pride, and determination. Blond hair had been permed at some point, giving it a ripple that stopped at her chin, where it was cut in a bob. Her jeans hugged her in a way that drew a man's attention to her hips and thighs. The plain white T-shirt under her denim jacket was probably meant to hide the curves under it, but it was no match for his skills at observation.

Now he knew why he'd remembered her. He'd felt this same jolt of attraction, this unexplainable urge to touch, when he'd watched her sitting on the bench in booking.

What a shame she had to be a fraud.

"I understand you two know each other." Singleton crossed the room and stood behind his desk in the position of power. "I also understand the circumstances weren't the best. I don't want to know the details. Whatever they were, you leave them at the door. Starting now, you focus on my daughter."

Griffin stayed where he was, to the left of the desk, leaving the woman in the middle of the carpet facing their joint scrutiny.

But somehow, she didn't look marooned or uncomfortable. "Fine with me," she said. She walked between them, hips swaying gently, and chose a wing chair by the window, which shrank their triangle, inverted it, and allowed her to invade the sacred space behind the desk. He watched

Jay discipline himself and not order her back to the rug like a disobedient puppy.

"Officer Knox," Tessa greeted him from her chair, as if the last time they'd met had been at an ice-cream social. She kicked off her slip-ons and tucked her feet up under her. A square of late-afternoon sun shone on her hair, lighting it and emphasizing the soft color of her skin. She settled into its warmth like a contented cat, and Griffin had a sudden vision of himself on his knees in front of the chair with his face in her lap.

God, where did that come from?

He shook off the image and took refuge behind cold formality. "Not anymore. It's just plain Griffin now. I invalided out a few years ago."

Some people would have said, "I'm sorry" or asked for details. Not this woman. She merely nodded and left his business to him.

Which was fine. He didn't want her in his business. Didn't want her in his head.

Didn't want her.

"Let me tell you how this is going to work," Singleton continued.

"I thought we already went through that." Tessa smiled at him, and even with all his defenses up, Griffin was taken aback at the sheer wattage of that smile. A deep dimple dented her right cheek and he felt his distrust waver.

All good cons had a great smile, he reminded himself harshly. Look at Ted Bundy.

"Yes, you made your position perfectly clear," Singleton said in a tone that told Griffin he wasn't over it yet.

"And what was that?" Griffin asked. Had that been the discussion in raised voices outside? Now he regretted his noble impulse not to eavesdrop.

"I just asked for a nurturing environment that would create a state of mind where I'm open to a vision," she said. "I also educated Mr. Singleton on how these things work."

"And how do these things work?" he asked. He'd bet his next paycheck she'd be rapping on tables and channeling Shirley MacLaine before the day was over.

She gave him a level glance. "Officer—Mr. Knox, that attitude is not helping. You may be a skeptic, but I'll ask you to keep your opinions to yourself while I'm here."

Spine. The lady had spine under those curves.

"I just asked how they worked. I need to be educated."

This time her gaze was a little scornful, a man-to-woman kind of look that made him realize he didn't want to admit weakness of any kind in front of her. "I have no doubt about that," she said in an innocent tone that communicated somehow that he was hopeless where women were concerned and probably hadn't had a date in ten years.

Ten months was more to the point, but—

Wait just a minute, here!

"I'm going to need a quiet place where I can work," she went on smoothly, turning to Singleton as if she hadn't just zinged Griffin right between the ribs. "And I'll need to spend a little time in your daughter's room, getting impressions of her, looking at pictures, that kind of thing. Once I'm in a state of openness, I'm able to tolerate very few interruptions, so I'll ask that your schedule impact me as little as possible."

"Ms. Nichols—"

"I won't isolate myself completely, of course. Contact with you and your household is necessary, so I'm fine with eating with the family or whatever."

This was too much for the control freak on a tight leash inside Jay Singleton. Griffin braced himself.

"You're welcome to eat with us," Singleton said in a hushed tone that told Griffin he was holding back a shout. "But as far as all this time alone, that's not possible."

"Why not?" Tessa inquired.

"Because I need some way of recording this information, of compiling it into a data set that we can use. I can't have you wandering around the house talking to yourself. What if we miss something?"

"Oh, I'll report in," Tessa said. She shifted so that her knees now pointed at Griffin. "And my memory is very good."

Singleton shook his head. "Not good enough."

She slid her feet off the chair and planted them on the floor. "We already discussed—"

Singleton rode right over her. "Every time you get data— a vision, voices in your head, whatever—I want someone there to hear it. And that someone is going to be Knox, here."

"What?" Both of them turned to stare at him.

Singleton nodded at Griffin, who glared at him. "You two are going to be joined at the hip. Griffin, I want you to take down everything she says, every detail, every description. All of it, no matter how nonsensical. We're talking 24/7. If she wakes up with a nightmare in the middle of the night, I want you there to listen. If she goes into a trance over her granola, you're going to write it down. Every time you get material, I want to know about it right away."

This was the most ridiculous waste of time Griffin had ever heard of. Not to mention completely unethical. "I'm not going to—"

"What do you mean, 24—"

Jay's glare was furious enough to silence them both. "If

we can get a jump on this character before he makes his ransom call, we can get Christina out of this before any harm comes to her or my ex-wife finds out she's gone. Clear?"

"No."

All Tessa's warm sensuality chilled as she got out of the chair and stalked to Jay's desk. Which was good. Griffin didn't need *that* to think about on top of this latest happy news.

"I told you what my abilities were, and what I need to be successful. Having *him*—" she flung a hand to the side to indicate Griffin without looking at him "—in my room at night, for God's sake, is not going to give me the environment I need."

"I don't care about your goddamn nurturing environment," Jay snapped. "I care about getting my daughter back, and right now you're holding us up!"

"Fine." She collected her handbag from the floor and tossed a smile at him as she headed for the door. "It's obvious you don't need me that badly. I quit. And I won't even charge you for my time or the mileage down here."

The flush of angry color had reached Jay's forehead— a sign his temper was about to blow. "Griffin, stop her!"

Accordingly, he ambled toward the door and reached out to take the girl's arm. She spun and his fingers grazed her skin.

"Going to try stuffing me in a police car again?" she asked with a dangerous light in her eye. He wouldn't put it past her to swing that handbag or stomp on his instep if he tried to get physical.

A sudden vision of her struggling in his arms, her breasts crushed against his chest and her thighs pushing against his, send a flash of heat searing through him.

"No." He stepped back to where it was safe, out of her space. "But don't go."

"Why shouldn't I? You don't trust me and he won't listen. How successful can this be?"

She was right on both counts, but it wasn't his job to say so. "Think of it from his point of view," he said in a tone too low for Jay to hear. "He's frustrated, things are out of control, and he's terrified. Give the guy a break."

"He needs to give me a break. Or I walk."

"I'll talk to him."

"Really." She narrowed her eyes and tilted her head, as if she were measuring him up against some invisible standard. "The minute I start feeling uncomfortable, I'm out of here."

"Suit yourself. But give it a chance first."

Give it a chance? Was he nuts? He was the last person who would give a psychic a chance or put the least amount of stock in anything she said. How had he found himself in the position of advocating for her?

Fifteen minutes later, when he'd calmed Jay enough so that the angry color had faded from his face and his boss could be rational, he was still wondering.

5

THIS IS A MISTAKE.

Tessa's backless tennies slapped on the marble as she followed the Latina in the black slacks and white shirt up the spiral staircase. She tried to convince herself that a fast dash for the Mustang and a quick escape were not the professional thing to do while every instinct she had was hollering, *Betrayal!* and *Danger!*

So what was she doing? Meekly trailing after the maid—sorry, Lucia—like an obedient child while a human thundercloud clomped up the steps behind her.

The 24/7 plan had been discarded, but she still had to deal with the twelve or eighteen or however many hours a day he was going to shadow her.

The back of her neck and the skin down her spine prickled, and she was intensely aware of the sway of her hips as she climbed each step. From prior experience she knew that meant someone was watching her—in this case, that Griffin Knox was eyeing her butt. She was under surveillance, plain and simple. She'd be lucky if she got to brush her teeth and go to the bathroom by herself. As soon as she could, she was going to sit down with Mr. Closed-Up-Fort-Knox and set a few simple ground rules, because the sooner she defined "personal privacy" for him, the better.

Family pictures, mostly of Christina, were framed on

the walls of the hallway down which Lucia led them. An internal urge prompted Tessa to study them, and she resolved to do that as soon as she found out where they were going.

There were four closed doors in this wing. Lucia opened the last door on the left. "I hope you will be comfortable here, Ms. Nichols."

"Thank you." She smiled at the young woman as she passed her, then stopped and blinked.

She'd been given a corner room, which meant windows on two sides, which meant a wraparound view of the Pacific, the beach, and the lawn below. "Holy cats." This was supposed to help her concentrate? She had pictured darkness and soft cushions and candles. An environment that included Christina. Not this stark brilliance where nothing was left in doubt. This was all wrong.

The walls were pale blue and the thick carpeting a soft oyster-gray. Matching blue drapes formed swags between sets of windows. Her rolling suitcase sat on its wheels at the end of a king-size bed. Robin, it appeared, had managed to get half his job done. She was just going to have to undo it all, and the person to start with was probably Lucia.

She heard the door close, and turned to stop Lucia from leaving. But Griffin Knox leaned on the door and crossed his arms. One side of his mouth turned up in an insincere smile.

"Alone at last," he said.

What was he still doing here?

"I figured we should take this opportunity to get a few things straightened out," he went on.

"I'm totally clear on what I'm supposed to do." She grabbed the handle of her suitcase and rolled it toward the door. "If you're not, you'd better talk to Mr. Singleton."

"Speaking of Jay, it'll be interesting to see what kind of hocus-pocus you plan on laying on him."

If anyone was going to do the straightening out, it would be her. "I don't plan on anything," she said evenly. She sat on the bed and gazed at him. "Whatever is going to come to me comes when it wants."

"So you say. But since no one can see inside your head, you can pretty much say what you want for sixty bucks an hour, can't you?"

She tipped her head to one side, as if that would help her to see him better. But all she saw was a long-legged, blue-eyed man with strong hands, a long jaw, and a mouth made for sin. He made a very sexy picture—if you liked the type and didn't count the distrust hovering around him.

"You know, I have a lot more reason to dislike you than you have to dislike me," she pointed out with a reasonable attempt at calm. "After all, I'm the one who got arrested."

He stared at her. "What are you talking about? I don't dislike you. I don't trust you. I think you're a fraud. But I don't dislike you."

She shook her head. "Not true." She paused, sorting through impressions taking shape in her mind. "It has to do with your mom, doesn't it? Do I look like her or something?"

He pushed himself off the back of her door and stalked to the window, where the percussive sound of the breakers boomed just below hearing range and reverberated under her ribs.

"Let me tell you how it's going to be." His shoulders were rigid under his shirt and she made a mental note not to bring up the subject of his mother again.

The shoulders were very nice, though, some part of her

noted. As was the rest of the rear view. Some men wore jeans as though they were a second skin—a soft, worn skin that moved and breathed and told you everything you wanted to know about the fine structure underneath. Griffin Knox, black cloud of disbelief that he was, was one of those men.

Oops, he was talking again. Pity.

"You're right, I arrested you for fraudulent activity two years ago, and I don't imagine you've changed your stripes since then. Your sister got you out of the charge, but I still believe you were involved in that whole Solstice Festival scam. So don't believe for one minute that I'm going to fall for it like those little old ladies getting their palms read."

"I don't read p—"

"Since I won't be around while you sleep, if you don't mind having your visions during day shift we'll both be happy."

"It's not something I can contr—"

"In the meantime, I'll take you to Christina's cottage because he's expecting it, not because I think you'll get anything more from the crime scene than I—"

She shot off the bed. "Would you stop interrupting me!"

Thankfully, he said nothing, just leveled another granite glare at her.

"First of all," she said clearly, before he opened his mouth again, "the thought of you anywhere near me at night gives me the creeps. Second of all, I've explained twice now that I need a safe, nurturing environment to open myself up in, and I am not getting it in this room or in present company. I need to be somewhere connected with Christina. Third, if there was some kind of scam going on at that festival, I was not involved in it and you have no right to convict me on no evidence, thank you very much. So if I can put aside the way you manhandled me and falsely accused me, then you can put aside your suspicions and just get over it, okay?"

"I do not convict people on no evidence," he said through his teeth.

Blood raced through her veins, powered by her pounding heart. Her breath was short, hot color came and went in her cheeks—classic "fight or flight" symptoms. She was dancing with danger here, and it was giving her an endorphin high.

Or something was. Something was driving her to challenge him, some reckless impulse that made her push him to see if she could get a bolt of lightning out of the thundercloud.

"If we are going to be stuck with each other until we find Christina, you will keep your opinions to yourself and do your job as recording secretary while I do mine." She stepped into his personal space and felt a ripple of satisfaction when he moved one window's width away. He pretended it was to open it, but she knew better. No problem. He could let the universe in if he wanted. It was on her side.

"Recording secretary." His voice was muffled with disgust. "My job is to find evidence, not babysit a fake psychic."

"I'm not a psychic, fake or otherwise. I'm a sensitive." He shrugged, clearly not interested in the distinction, but she plowed on anyway. "I see things sometimes, like when I saw Christina tied up with the scarves, but mostly I get impressions from people's possessions or photographs."

"Impressions about their possessions." He smiled, another humorless facial movement. "And how to get your hands on them, right?"

She didn't bite. "I don't have telekinetic powers or a big suitcase, so you can get that out of your head. I don't read minds, I don't bend spoons, and I don't see dead people. I don't deal well with sarcasm—and authority figures make me twitch."

"That's a lot of don'ts. So what do you do?"

"I connect," she told him simply. "That's why it's important that I go to Christina's room. I'm probably going to need to sleep there, too, because there is nothing in here—" she glanced from the ceiling to him to the floor "—that's going to help."

"Not gonna happen." He registered the subtle insult and his body radiated resistance, as though he were personally going to guard the place before she burgled it.

"It has to happen if I'm going to do my job." She got off the bed and rolled her suitcase to the door. "I'll ask Lucia to show me the way."

He had to hustle to beat her to it, and they both reached for the door handle at the same time. His hand covered hers and pressed it into the antique china ball, and a *zing!* of sensation whipped up her arm. He jerked back as if he'd been burned and she took the opportunity to slip past him and out the door.

The sound of her suitcase's wheels on the Mexican slate brought Lucia out of one of the rooms, and in the end it was Griffin who brought up the rear as Tessa explained what she needed and they trooped down the stairs.

Which would have made her feel triumphant except for the fact that, once again, he was staring at her butt.

TESSA TOOK ONE LOOK at the cottage and knew this was the place where she needed to stay.

The problem was convincing everyone else.

They'd picked up Jay Singleton on the way down the stairs, so the two men least likely to promote a calm, nurturing atmosphere accompanied her out to the little Spanish casita on the other side of a flagstone patio off the main house. When Singleton forged ahead and reached for the wrought-iron door handle, Tessa stopped him.

"Mr. Singleton, if you don't mind, I'd like to go in alone. First impressions matter."

She heard Griffin Knox mutter "I'll keep an eye on her," as if she were an ex-con likely to make off with the silver, and resolutely blocked him out. She wanted to go in here like an empty slate so the impressions she got would have more impact. In fact—

"The two of you need to stay outside." She parked her suitcase beside a butterfly bush and put one hand on the door handle. "I can't work if your influence is interfering with hers."

"Now, wait just a minute," Griffin began, but Singleton held up a hand and cut him off.

"We'll stay right here." He indicated the step. "But I want to be able to hear what you have to say."

"Fair enough. Just don't come into the room." Tessa blocked them both out and focused her concentration on what lay ahead as she pushed open the door.

Color first: purple bedspread, gray walls, black furniture, all at odds with pale paint and the white light streaming in the windows.

Then scent: a protein bar left on the dresser, cosmetics, something heavy and musky—ah, perfume. Plants everywhere, giving off a rich scent of soil and green leaves.

Then details: college applications, all blank, tossed on a desk. A printer on the floor. A walk-in closet on the opposite side. A stuffed toy between the pillows.

She picked up the glass bottle of perfume on the vanity table, then looked at her reflection in the mirror. Tucked into the sides of it were snapshots of Christina—she recognized the dark eyes and wide mouth from her initial vision—with various people, including two girls around the same age. Tessa reached out and touched one showing Christina with a tall, dark-eyed woman.

"She's homesick," Tessa said slowly. "She misses her mom and nana. That's part of the reason why she won't pick a college. She doesn't want to commit to living out here."

She didn't turn to see how her words were received. Instead, she moved toward the closet. Clothes were the most intimate part of a person's environment. Besides what they told you themselves about the subject, impressions remained, hanging around them like old perfume.

Tessa studied the tops and dresses hanging on the rods, and the pants and sweaters stacked in cubes on one wall of the walk-in. She had no idea if Christina had duplicates at her mother's home, but there were enough clothes here to keep a couple of teenagers going for a year. After a few moments, it became clear there was a change in the wardrobe. There were the usual sporty things suitable for days at the beach, school clothes and sloppy things to hang around the house with. Then there were clubby things with spaghetti straps and without, black jersey galore, spandex, even rhinestones. High-end labels with a few price tags still on the pieces. But what was this?

She touched one of the dresses, a taupe jersey, and a defiant voice clearly said in her head: *Do you see me now? Will this make you look?*

O-o-o-kay. So, was this the kind of thing you reported to a teenager's father?

"She wants somebody's attention," she called finally, her voice muffled in the depths of the closet.

"What?" Singleton's voice came from the doorway, impatiently.

Tessa walked to the closet door and craned around the corner until she could see the two men still standing obediently on the mat.

"She's trying to get someone's attention," she repeated. "Someone older, I think. A man."

Singleton swore. "Who?"

Tessa shook her head. "Don't know. It could be you, for all I know. But the clothes she's using are pretty revealing, so I doubt it."

"The kidnapper, maybe?" Griffin put in. "In most abduction cases the perpetrator is someone the victim knows."

Tessa considered this. "It's impossible to say. But we can keep it in mind."

"Anything else?" Singleton wanted to know.

"Not from first impressions. That's why I'm going to stay here. Sometimes these things work in layers. Once the first layer says what it has to, the other layers get a chance."

Out of the corner of her eye, she saw Griffin clench his jaw, as though biting back what he wanted to say. Unfortunately, the message his body language sent came through loud and clear: *I don't believe one word.*

Too bad. Jay Singleton believed her, and his was the only opinion she cared about.

Really. If all she ever saw in Griffin Knox's eyes was contempt and disbelief, that was fine with her. His opinions were totally irrelevant.

Singleton had just processed what she'd said. "Stay here?" he repeated. "I thought a room had been made up for you at the house."

Tessa braced herself. So much for believing in her. Maybe it had its limits. "You think I brought my suitcase all the way over here because I'm attached to it?" With no help from any of the males present.

Clearly, Jay didn't get rhetorical questions. "No, I thought you had equipment in it or something. You can't stay in my daughter's cottage. It's out of the question."

"Can you think of a better place for me to get impressions of her, to listen to what her living space has to tell me?"

"You'll have access to it anytime you want. But you're not sleeping here."

"Why not?"

Jay stared at her as if the last time someone had questioned one of his edicts was in the previous century. Maybe it had been. "Because I said so."

In spite of herself, she laughed, and the color mounted in his cheeks. "You sound like such a dad." Then she sobered. "But I'm not a child. I'm being paid to do a job, and this is how I'm going to do it. Something inside me is urging me to stay here."

Go on, argue with that one.

"I'll keep an eye on her, boss," Griffin said.

"Oh, you will, will you?" she demanded. "Do you think I'm going to make off with her jewelry or something? Can I remind you that most business relationships are based on trust? So far I'm the only one doing any of that around here."

Singleton rubbed his face and sighed.

She sensed victory only seconds away, if she could keep her temper and resist the childish urge to throw the glass perfume bottle at Griffin Knox's head. "I know you're only thinking about Christina's feelings, about me invading her privacy," she said to Jay. "But I'm not going to go through her drawers. I need a place to get close to her, and this is the place. Nowhere else is going to work half as well."

"You're right," he said at last. "Fine. We'll deal with Christina's feelings when she gets home. For now, do what you have to do."

"Thank you."

Singleton nodded, then turned and strode across the patio and out of sight, leaving her alone with Fort Knox. She moved around the living room/bedroom combination, carefully keeping her back to him. Not that it made a bit of difference. A tingle began between her shoulder blades, right about the place where his gaze was probably boring a hole in her T-shirt.

Keeping an eye on her, indeed.

"Why do you come up with this stuff?" he said from his post by the door. "Just to upset the guy?" He leaned casually on the wall, but his tone was anything but casual.

"What stuff? You mean, about staying here?"

"Yeah. That and the thing about the person whose attention Christina wants. Stuff that's hard for a father to hear."

For a moment, Tessa debated the wisdom of defending her gift to someone who so obviously discounted it. But this was a cop. Maybe if she talked to him the way she talked to Linn, she could at least get through.

"It isn't groundless." She touched the untidy stack of college applications. "And he wants to know everything, upsetting or not, which is why he's letting me stay here." She glanced at the closet. "As for this mystery person, you'll see a change in the kind of clothes she's buying. The things she's bought recently—with the tags still on them—

are very adult. The kind of clothes that are designed to get attention. And it's clear she wants that attention to be male."

Griffin crossed the room and leaned on the wall just inside the closet, next to a rack of shoes. She moved past him and lifted the taupe jersey dress off the rail by its hanger. "Look at this one, for instance. Spaghetti straps, backless, with a built-in bra that could hold back the American River. Dolce & Gabbana's done some serious engineering here for the purpose of capturing a man's attention and holding it."

"Are you so good at knowing what holds a man's attention?"

"Well, I'm betting we're talking about a man who needs youth—young body, young skin, young attitude. Who picks a girl who won't judge him because she's not very experienced yet. And the more I think about it, the more I wonder if you weren't right about him and the kidnapper being the same person." Tessa stopped, suddenly realizing what he'd asked. "Was that a personal comment?"

"Take it however you want."

"What I want isn't relevant. What you meant is."

She couldn't read his expression, but there was an odd, heated light in his eyes.

"I was just curious," he said. "Just wanted to confirm you can't read a man's mind. When you're in bed with him, for instance."

6

GRIFFIN WATCHED SHOCK, then confusion, then challenge ripple across her expression. He didn't know why he was goading her. He was supposed to be watching out for his boss's interests, waiting for her to slip up and show herself to be a fraud.

Unfortunately, all she was showing was a damn good grasp of human behavior and a skill at observation that was as good as his.

Better, even. He hadn't even thought about what sales tags meant on a woman's clothes. What he *was* thinking about was what the dress on the hanger would look like on Tessa. How the smooth fabric would look against her fair skin. And what kind of spectacular results the designer's engineering would produce if it cupped breasts like hers.

"Of course not," she said. "Who wants to hear a whole lot of mental grunting, anyway?"

Stop fantasizing about her breasts, you idiot.

"Maybe you ought to pick a different kind of guy," he suggested. "One who thinks in sentences."

She turned her back on him, which, he was discovering, was how she communicated she'd been offended.

"You know, we have to work together for however many days this takes," she said from the other side of the room.

"You might consider being civil and keeping this on a business, not a personal, level."

She was right. How could he fantasize about her on one level and label her a criminal on another? What kind of man did that make him?

The truth was, he simply wasn't ready for her to be right and for him to be wrong.

"I know you don't believe in me, and that's fine," she went on. "My sister doesn't, either. But I do have something to contribute, and if you'll let me do my job maybe it will make it easier for you to do yours."

Right again. He hated that.

"So can we please call a truce and get on with it?"

To remind himself he was a decent guy, he kept his gaze on her face. Her eyes were just as wide and blue as he remembered from two years ago, and the short haircut accentuated her pointed chin and terrific cheekbones. And that mouth with its full lower lip and dented upper—

No, don't think about her mouth, either. Besides, how could such reasonable things come out of it one minute and such nutty things the next?

Was that his problem? He couldn't figure out whether she was a nut, a criminal, or for real. A fair man would give her a chance to prove herself one way or another. And he prided himself on being a fair man. The way he was treating her was out of character for him—had been from the moment he'd remembered who belonged to the voice on the phone.

He didn't like being out of character. He was comfortable in his own skin these days and didn't much care for anything that scratched at it—the way this woman seemed to do without even trying.

"Okay," he said finally. He ambled over to where she

stood by Christina's window, looking out toward the beach. "Truce it is." He paused, in case she wanted to respond to that, but she didn't. "What do you see out there?"

"I was just wondering if she could have gone that way." Her tone was back to being calm, as if she'd accepted his agreement and moved on immediately.

"I thought of that, too. But too much time has gone by. The beach is too public for any one set of tracks to tell us anything. Too many dogs being walked, kids playing, people jogging."

"She liked the beach." Her tone was soft, intense, as if she were puzzling her way toward something. "That's why she insisted on this cottage, I think, instead of staying in the house. So she could feel more a part of it."

"You can tell this just by touching things. So you're a psychometrist?"

She shrugged. "If that's what they call it. I don't go around labeling myself. When I touch something, the experience is usually intense and realistic. I can get lost in the moment, the way a person does in a really gripping movie, but I stay myself." She glanced at him. "I use cards, sometimes, too, for direction."

Cards? Like tarot? Never mind. He didn't want to know any of these details. "Good call on the clothes thing." Though God knows how he could use that information. Was this a kidnapping or something else? Could Christina have run away? Where? And with whom?

"It helps to be a woman in another woman's closet."

She smiled, and he realized he was standing far too close—close enough to smell some whiff of jasmine he supposed must be shampoo. Hmm. She had pretty hair. So soft that it made you want to brush it away from her face. Cup her chin. Raise her mouth to yours—

Would you stop?

He moved away. "If we're done here, I think you wanted to have a look at the photos in the upstairs hall, right?" He hardly waited to hear her murmur of agreement before he hotfooted it back to the house.

TESSA GAVE HER HEAD a shake as if to clear it, then brought her suitcase in, parked it next to the bed, closed the door of the cottage behind her and followed him across the lawn. He was a hard man to figure out. One minute antagonistic, one minute rational, the next minute hightailing it out of there as if his butt was on fire. And for what reason? She hadn't said anything remotely offensive or scary—in fact, she'd made a considerable personal sacrifice to be civil.

Men. No wonder the cards always said "not yet." She should be grateful.

There was no one in the hallway when she let herself into the house, but on the left, behind the oak slab of his office door, she heard Singleton's muffled shouting in what sounded like a mixture of English and Mandarin. The sound followed her upstairs until it was lost at the turn where the hallway began.

Griffin was standing about halfway along, looking the pictures over as if to find a suitable one for her to start with.

"This is Christina's mother." He stood aside so she could look at the picture of the dark-haired woman on the sailboat. Her head was thrown back as she gripped one of the sheets, and she was laughing.

"She's very pretty. Christina looks like her." The taupe jersey dress could have been made for a brown-eyed brunette.

He glanced at her. "How did you—? Oh, in the cottage. The pictures in the mirror."

"No, I saw her before, remember? In my first vision."

"Right." With a definite air of "I'm not touching that one," he moved farther along the hallway. "Here's a recent one."

Christina's graduation picture. Slowly, Tessa raised her hand and touched the glass that covered the photograph. She waited for that shift in reality, that sense of the tangible world fading slightly, that would tell her she could read something from the picture, but nothing happened.

He was standing too close. She moved casually down the row of photographs, moving backward in time until it ended with a ponytailed cherub in first grade. Still, no matter how often she moved, there he was, right beside her. In the deserted hall, she became increasingly aware of the power of him, of the sense that he was at ease in his own body despite the slight hitch in his stride.

"Anything?" Griffin asked.

"No." She cleared her throat. "Sometimes it works, sometimes it doesn't. You never know until you try."

"So that's what you want me to report to Jay? That it didn't work?"

Tessa looked at him, a little surprised. "I didn't promise that it would. We did pretty well for my first day here. We know she was trying to impress someone. We have one possibility—that the someone and the kidnapper are the same person." She paused. "At this point in any good mystery, the cop goes off and compiles a list of all the victim's known associates to see if anyone fits either profile."

"Already done." Griffin's tone was flat. "Unfortunately, because Jay is so set on secrecy, we can't call anyone to see if they know anything. And before you ask—" he held up a hand "—she didn't keep a diary or a calendar. That would be way too organized."

Okay, so maybe it was a mistake expecting a real cop to behave like the ones in books. But did he have to be quite so negative? Not to mention so tall and distracting? And did he have to give off this sense that he was waiting for something to happen? What?

She took refuge in speculation—stream-of-consciousness chatter that would put words, if nothing else, between them. "Surely her dad knows one or two of her friends well enough to ask them to keep it quiet. Maybe Christina confided in them about who she wanted to impress when they were shopping."

"Right, and teenage girls are going to tell an authority figure anything? Or do what he asks them?"

"Probably not." Then an idea struck her. "But they might tell me."

"Tell you what?"

At the sound of the woman's voice on the landing, both of them turned. "Hey, Mandy," Griffin said, and the atmosphere of anticipation dissipated. "You haven't met Tessa Nichols yet, have you?"

The blonde held out a hand and looked Tessa in the eye. "Not yet. I figured Jay was enough for anyone to start with. Nice to meet you, Tessa."

The woman's grip was warm and firm and her self-control was admirable. But the worry was there in her eyes and in the tight grip of her hand.

"We'll find her," Tessa said quietly. "We've already made some progress."

Griffin looked from one to the other, obviously a little confused at what must look like a sudden change in subject.

"You get right to the point, don't you? What kind of progress?" Mandy asked. Her clear gaze never left Tessa's face. She tugged, and Tessa released her hand.

Griffin outlined what little they had, and ended by saying, "This is just guesswork, Mandy. I'd rather have something concrete to tell you."

"We don't have anything concrete," she reminded him, and led the way back out to the landing. "That's why Tessa is working with us. I'll take whatever we can get, personally. Are you going to tell Jay?"

"He wants reports."

"Hourly?"

"Almost."

"Oh, good. You can give them to *me* hourly." She grinned at him as though they'd been best friends for years.

Maybe they had. But there was nothing sexual in their camaraderie. The impression that had flashed in Tessa's mind during their handshake—under the fear—had been one of clarity and warmth. This woman had it all—married to one of the ten richest men in the country, a house in Carmel, a face and figure to die for—and a loving heart to boot. Tessa devoutly hoped that Jay knew how lucky he was.

"Mandy, do you think Jay could call some of Christina's friends?"

She lifted an eyebrow. "Are you kidding? He doesn't even know who the neighbors are, much less who his daughter hangs out with. Why? Do you think one of them might know something?"

"It's possible she might have let something slip," Tessa explained. "Some clue about anyone new she might have met lately—because obviously it wasn't in a family situation—or what plans she might have had."

"She likes two of the girls at Pebble Beach. I play tennis with the mother of one of them. But there's a problem."

"What's that?" Griffin asked.

"Jay has told me he wants this kept quiet. With the media gathering for the PGA event this weekend, I think the risk is too great if we started calling around and people put two and two together."

A muscle flexed in Griffin's jaw. "Can you get around it somehow? Find out without them figuring out why you want to know?"

"Oh, right," Mandy scoffed. "Slide a lie about her friend past a teenager? That'll be a huge success."

"So bottom line, we're on our own," he said grimly. "He's got my hands tied from every direction. How am I supposed to find her if he closes off every road I try to take?"

"Think of it from his side," Mandy said. "He's spent the last ten years since his breakup with Barbara trying to get more than alternate holidays with his kid. Now that Christina's old enough to choose him, he's not going to do anything to jeopardize the status quo with Barbara." She lowered her voice, and Griffin and Tessa both leaned closer. "Because, you see, if she gets her degree out here and not Boston, she makes her networks and connections here. That makes her more likely to get a job here, meet someone, and make a life on his side of the country. See where I'm going with this?"

Griffin straightened. "Please tell me Jay isn't screwing up my investigation so that he'll be in the same state as his future grandchildren." His tone said, *Just shoot me now*.

"You know Jay." Mandy smiled at him, but behind the smile was understanding and the shadow of her own fear. "Always thinking in the long term."

"I'll do everything I can to help," Tessa said into the silence.

"I know you will." Mandy nodded. "But in the meantime, I came to find you for a reason. Dinner is at six in the dining room." She waved into the echoing space of the entry hall below them, in the direction of a door on the far side. "Right there, in case Griffin hasn't given you the entire tour."

Six. An hour away. "If you guys have other things to do, I'll just wander around and look at pictures. You never know what might spark something."

"Then I guess I'm wandering with you," Griffin said.

So much for subtle hints.

Mandy clattered down the stairs and left her alone again with Griffin. As he stood next to her, she could smell the freshly laundered cotton of his T-shirt and the faint scent of coffee. His thumbs were hooked loosely in his front pockets, his long fingers resting lightly on worn denim. The pose masked any tension he might be feeling, instead projecting a kind of casual masculinity that drew the eye right between his hands.

She would *not* look at his button-fly Levi's. So what if his hips were lean and his legs long and rangy. He was an ex-cop, and cops had fallen off the bottom of her list long ago.

She tried to concentrate on the pictures in the second hallway, which, from the look of the bedrooms, was where the family slept. Here the pictures were a mix of family events, where Mandy's smile was most evident, business successes, and holidays in places where there were palm trees or endless slopes of snow. Some of the photographs even featured Griffin in the background.

The man whose body heat she could feel against her bare arm at this moment, whose gaze felt the way his hand might if it were memorizing the contours of her body.

Oh, come on. Your imagination is running away with you. You cannot feel a man's gaze.

Maybe most people couldn't, but she could. Right now.

If he didn't stop looking at her breasts she was going to cross her arms, and that would make her look defensive and prudish, and that would seriously annoy her.

You're imagining it because he's standing so close.

Was he trying to intimidate her? If so, he was going to fail. It was perfectly clear that she and her talent were all he had to work with, so that put her in control—a feeling so unusual that she was going to enjoy the novelty of it for all it was worth.

No matter where he happened to be looking. In fact, let him look. He could look, but he couldn't touch. She straightened her shoulders and sensed more than saw him rocking back on his heels. Ha.

She stopped in front of a picture that looked as though it had been taken at a Christmas costume party. The internal sensor she had learned to trust over the years went, *What's this?*

"That was taken here at the house last Christmas," Griffin said in the carefully resigned tone of a tour guide. "There's a ballroom downstairs, on the ocean side."

There were a number of costumed people in the photo, including Jay Singleton as Santa and his daughter as something in a diaphanous dress with silvery wings. A sugarplum fairy, maybe? Singleton had his arms around a couple of guys in Roman togas, while a third guy raised a tall glass in a toast. Tessa could only imagine how romantic a winter dance in such a beautiful setting might be, with French doors opening on the terrace and the sea crashing in the background. Ah, the life of the rich and famous.

On the down side, these people had their kids stolen. Given the option, she would rather be a nobody and safe in student housing than the daughter of one of the ten richest men in the country, tied up on a bed with scarves.

7

From the private journal of Jay Singleton

SHE SAYS THAT Christina was trying to impress someone. An older man, she thinks.

That's bloody impossible. The only things Christina cares about are shopping, clothes, and a hundred and one ways to avoid filling out college applications. Tessa says she doesn't want to commit. I don't get it. If moving out here isn't a commitment then what is?

Unless she didn't really want to come. But she wasn't forced. I stated my case, told her I wanted her to come live with me. I may have told her I loved her; in fact, I'm sure I must have. That isn't forcing anybody.

Then why the hell didn't she want to commit? And speaking of committing, who is this older man?

I'm getting that urge to hurt something again. Time to go whack a bucket of golf balls or go out to my secret log pile behind the garage and chop wood. Screw the shrinks—chopping wood is the best therapy I know. A big axe, lots of violence and it lets you think at the same time.

I can't think of a single person Christina has ever shown an attraction to. We have parties here, she talks to everyone—or more to the point, no one. She speaks when spoken to and the rest of the time she looks out the window as if she can't wait to get out of there. I used to think she hated hanging around with us fuddy-duddies, but now with this older man thing I'm not so sure. What if she was looking out the window at the driveway, waiting for his car?

What older man?

This is gonna drive me stark-raving mad.

Tessa said it might be me, but probably not. Why is Christina trying to get attention? I practically work from home so I'll be here for her. We eat supper together every night. How much more attention does a girl need? Does she want me to take her on a trip or something? I have to go to Singapore anyway—maybe she'd like shopping on Orchard Street. It would be pure purgatory for me, but I'd make the sacrifice.

If she'd just come home.

GRIFFIN WRAPPED UP the day's details with Jay Singleton over dinner, though *details* was a bit of a stretch. Singleton seemed satisfied, though, which surprised the hell out of Griffin. But then, if you had no clues at all, a theory was better to go on than nothing.

He suggested hitting up Christina's gal pals at the country club for information, but none of them could figure out how to do it without alerting the immediate world that she was missing. At least it was a possibility, as soon as someone came up with a story that would work.

After dinner, Tessa declined the offer of drinks. "I'm going to the cottage," she said. "Since she vanished during the night maybe it will help to see things at that time, from her perspective."

Which sounded like total B.S. to Griffin, but his job was to shadow her, so shadow her he would.

The wisteria vine shading the patio outside the cottage

created wavering trails of shadow on the flagstones as they crossed to the front door. The night was damp, and he breathed in the scent of freshly cut grass and the perfume of the purple wisteria, mixed with the tang of seaweed washed up on the beach several hundred yards away. The marine layer sitting offshore breathed cool air ahead of itself as it moved in for the night, giving relief from the heat of Indian summer.

The scents of the night, the quiet, the sensuous sway of the woman walking ahead of him…at any other time this would be a perfect setting for a night of lovemaking.

He shook off the thought. The night was creating a false sense of intimacy, that was all. This sense of waiting, of anticipation created by the wash of waves in the distance and the sweet scent of flowers, was just an illusion. The only thing he was waiting for was some kind of information provided by Jay's rent-a-mystic, here. That was it.

It was strange how confidently she moved in the dark, though. Had she memorized the place when they'd been here earlier?

"Want me to stay on the step again?" His voice sounded rough in the breathing silence, even to him.

She glanced over her shoulder at him as she pushed open the door. "No, it's okay. Don't turn on the lights, though."

"Why not?"

"Sometimes you can see better in the dark."

O-o-o-kay. *You* in this case obviously did not mean him. He preferred light. Clarity. Facts. Things that could be catalogued and checked into an evidence locker, things that didn't lie or hold double meanings.

He moved cautiously behind her, expecting at any moment to stub a foot on a table leg or run into a chair. The moon had not risen yet, but still, a little silvery light filtered in through the windows, just enough so that he could see her moving softly, slowly, touching things as she had before. Just a light caress of the fingers, one that gently asked, *Do you have anything for me?*

He wondered if she touched her boyfriend like that after she hadn't seen him for a while. *Do you have anything for me?* Because of course she had a boyfriend. A woman whose hips swayed like that and who could make a man think about falling on his knees and nuzzling her just by the simple act of sitting down surely had to.

Too bad the guy, whoever he was, was going to have to do without her until they found Christina. Too bad he couldn't enjoy the sight of that sweet, pear-shaped derriere or that dimpled smile. Griffin had spent the whole time in the upstairs hallway trying to imagine what her breasts would look like without the confines of bra and T-shirt. Would they be perky and pointed? Or lush and full? This unknown guy, damn him, already knew the exact color of her nipples, and whether she had large areolas or small.

He was betting small, with hard nipples a man could roll on his tongue like ripe raspberries, making her moan when he sucked—

"—know if she had any special possession?"

Griffin came out of his fantasy with a start. Thank God she'd kept the lights off, because he definitely didn't want her to see what was happening in his pants while he stood watching her.

"What?"

"I said, do you know if she was attached to a special possession? A toy, a necklace, something like that?"

He was having a little difficulty making the shift from

thinking about an adult woman's body to random possessions. "Damned if I know."

He heard her sigh. "Never mind. I thought all cops had photographic memories like my sister, but evidently not."

There was nothing wrong with his memory, once something registered. And a young woman's stuff did not register unless it had been stolen or sent to the anxious parents with a ransom note.

"Can we turn on the lights?"

"You might as well," she said from the vicinity of Christina's vanity table. "It looks like I'm going to have to go through her things after all."

He turned to find a wall switch and ran his foot into something solid sitting next to the bed. "Damn! I just found your suitcase."

"And I found a switch."

He heard a click and the room was illuminated by the mirror on the vanity, which was one of those theater-type ones with lightbulbs all around it. Tessa leaned on her hands, gazing into the mirror as though she could see through it to something beyond, like Alice and the looking glass.

His gaze stalled on the gentle angle her body drew, from lower back to derriere to thigh. Her breasts swayed forward, creating another deep curve, the kind that begged to be followed with the hands.

Griffin's body tightened and he glanced away—at the ceiling, at the closet, at the window—anywhere but at Tessa.

"What do you have to tell me? Oh." Her voice trailed away, as though she'd come around a corner and the view had stopped her cold.

"Tessa?" She didn't reply. Cautiously, he moved to the

end of the bed and sank onto it, watching her from a couple of feet away. "You okay?"

"Touch me," she whispered into the mirror.

That was *not* what he'd expected her to say. In fact, he'd probably misheard her. "What?"

"She wants him to look at her," she said, her voice soft and far away.

Was she talking to him? Had she seen the boner in his pants? Griffin sat frozen, as though a spotlight had come on and caught him in the act of lusting after her. This was bad. He couldn't start anything with her—he didn't trust her. Hell, he didn't even like her. Not that liking someone had anything to do with this balled-up investigation. Under other circumstances, maybe, he might act on the messages his body was sending him, but not with a woman who could—

"She says, 'I'm right in front of you, but all you see is what you want to see. Not the real me, the one who wants you.'"

With a sudden jolt, he knew.

She doesn't care about you, you idiot—she's telling you about Christina!

He'd seen plenty of strange things in his career, but this really rang the bell on the Weird Shit-O-Meter.

"She even bought a new dress," she said to her reflection. "The taupe one, because he told her he liked it in the shop. It makes her look at least five years older. And it does fabulous things for her. You know—here." She straightened.

Griffin almost swallowed his tongue as her hands cupped her breasts and lifted them the way that dress might. His body leaped in response to the seductive movement while his common sense shouted that it wasn't—couldn't be—personal.

Gathering what was left of his fried brain cells, he asked softly, "Where is she going to wear it?"

"Not around here," Tessa told him, and to his enormous relief, dropped her hands to her sides. "To the club in Santa Rita. He knows the guy working the door."

"Who?" Griffin asked.

"Don't know his name. He's at Atlantis. She likes to dance."

"No, I mean who knows the guy working the door?" Griffin held his breath. "Was he the guy who took Christina?"

"She lo-o-o-ves to dance."

Tessa raised her arms above her head and swiveled her hips, her feet moving to the beat of music he couldn't hear. He stared as she turned slowly, her hips undulating as smoothly as those of a belly dancer or one of those hip-hop stars on TV.

Think! Get some information before she comes out of it!

"Tessa, who does Christina go dancing with?" he asked urgently. "And who did she get a fake I.D. from?"

"Ashley and Melissa," she sang, ignoring his second question. "So smooth."

Griffin watched her, frustration and desire at war in his veins. Were you supposed to wake a sensitive out of a trance? It wasn't like sleepwalking, was it, where you could scare someone by waking them up?

He couldn't sit around and wait, either. It would take him a half hour to reach Santa Rita, giving him a few short hours to make inquiries before the club closed.

He got up and reached for one of her hands. "Tessa?"

She drew in a sharp breath and her dancing slowed to just a movement of her shoulders. "Yes, I'm here." Her voice was back to normal, with none of the breathy, dreamy quality it had held a moment ago.

"You had some kind of vision."

Simultaneously, they both realized he was still holding her hand. She smiled and twirled under his arm, as if they were swing dancing. "It was about the D and G dress and a club, right?"

He let go of her hand. "Yeah. The Atlantis. So…" How could he word this? Then he thought, *Look who you're talking to. Just spit it out.* "So were you channeling Christina, or what?"

"What's the matter? Don't feel like dancing?" When he didn't reply, she shook her head in mock regret. "Channeling isn't one of my gifts," she said. "I was, well, watching the playback of a memory would be a way to put it. Maybe she was rehearsing things she wanted to say to him. The man. Whoever he is."

Griffin felt a little lost. "This is way outside my experience," he said at last. "I don't even know how to reply to this." Not to mention the fact that he couldn't get the sight of her dancing out of his head. That sinuous movement, that invitation—

"Hey, we all have our gifts." She sounded as if she meant to comfort him or something. "But she's definitely keeping secrets from me. I couldn't pick up any names. Just Atlantis."

"Sure. Well." Back to the business of concrete facts. "I'm going to this club to see what I can get." He walked over and opened the door. The night breeze wafted in, carrying the scent of wisteria.

"Now?"

"Well, sure, now. Do you want me to sit around until it closes?"

"No, of course not."

"I'll show a picture to the bouncer at the door. I might get lucky and he'll tell me the name of this guy Christina's hung up on. Then I can go track him down. Whether he has anything to do with this or not, he's got to be able to give me some information."

"I'm coming with you."

"No, you're not."

"Maybe I'll pick something up there," she argued. "She had strong emotions about the Atlantis. That might work for me. Besides—" she took a couple of dance steps "—I still feel like dancing."

Well, he'd look a lot less like an investigator if she was there posing as his date. He just had to be careful to keep his focus on the job instead of this blond baggage whose dancing made him think about sex.

"All right," he said at last. "My truck's parked in the staff lot, right behind the main garage. I'll meet you there in ten minutes, after I brief Jay."

"You got it." She brushed past him and heaved her suitcase up onto the bed. Jasmine mixed with the scent of wisteria.

If someone had told him two days ago he'd be going clubbing with a psychic, he'd have told them where to put it. He had never been one of those people who wanted to know the future. The present and the prospect of a decent 401(k) were good enough for him.

A PICKUP TRUCK. She should have insisted that they take the Mustang; at least it had some style. Tessa sighed and climbed onto the running board. She parked her butt on the seat and then swung her legs into the cab. Complicated, yes, but better than the alternative, which was flashing everyone in sight.

Griffin looked at her a little strangely, then did a double take. "What the hell is that?"

"It's a skirt, obviously. Suede. I thought the fringe was cool. When I saw it at this secondhand shop I go to on P—"

"That isn't a skirt, that's a frigging Band-Aid! What are you trying to do? Turn this into a circus?"

"Oh, great." She tugged on the skirt and fastened the seat belt as he fired up the engine with a roar and wheeled out into the long driveway. "A zillion cops in the world and I get the one who's a father figure in training."

"What's that supposed to mean?"

Good thing she'd been hanging on to the armrest. If she hadn't, she might have bumped her head on the window as he took the first curve in the drive.

"That's the kind of thing dads say," she replied. "Well, not my dad. He's a 'live and let live' kind of guy. But most dads—Jay Singleton, for instance—would certainly say something like that."

"I am not a father figure!" he snapped. He gave the brakes a nominal tap and turned onto the main road.

"You don't have to get grouchy about it."

"I don't like being slotted into a role that has nothing to do with how I really am."

"Like what you've been doing to me this whole time? Gosh, I'm so sorry."

That stopped him. She probably sounded like a petulant teenager herself, but she couldn't help it. He may look like a beat-up warrior, but all this distrust and authority-figure stuff just rubbed her the wrong way. And when that happened, her filters went down and she said what she thought without considering anybody else's feelings.

"Besides, I wear what I want. Just because a woman

wears something that's fun and makes her feel sexy doesn't mean it's going to turn into a circus. Like men are going to lose control when they see it. I have more confidence in guys than that."

He just snorted and didn't reply until they were out on the highway. This beat-up old truck had one heck of an engine, and it was obviously in perfect running order. She couldn't see the speedometer, but they had to be doing nearly eighty.

"You're right," he said abruptly five or six miles later.

"What, about guys losing control at the sight of my skirt?"

"No. About what I'm doing. You said you weren't involved in that street fair episode and I didn't believe you."

"What did you think I'd done?"

He kept his eagle eye on the road, but his tone had lost the edge it usually had when he spoke to her. "There was a ring of small-time cons and scammers using the fair as a front for fraud."

She sat back. "Wow. No kidding."

"Turns out it was all the people selling herbal remedies in a cooperative. One of them said that you and the woman in the booth next to you were in on it, so I hauled you all in." He glanced at her. "You make an enemy there or something?"

She shrugged. "No idea. I got one of the better booths as far as placement goes, though. Maybe somebody got angry about it."

"Anyway, that's the story. Fraud is one of my hot buttons, and having you involved then and now just bent me out of shape."

Tessa's mind flashed to the first impression she'd received of him. She'd resolved not to bring it up again, but it had to be said. "It has something to do with your mom, doesn't it?"

He threw her a glance, then returned his gaze to the highway. They were nearly to the Santa Rita exit. "Keep that up and I'll start to believe you know what you're doing."

"Keep this up and you won't have to apologize for the circus remark."

The corners of his mouth twitched, and then he sobered. "My mom's getting old and she lives on her own. She's pretty sharp, but women in that age group are targets for a certain kind of character. When I was still with the P.D. she hired this handyman to do some stuff around the house. He came off as Mr. Trustworthy and soon he was giving her financial advice and before I knew what was going on, he'd talked her into giving him access to her accounts. I think he even had her convinced they were going to get married. Anyhow, she dropped something in conversation one day and I made it to the bank just in time. He was in the process of cleaning out her savings account, after he'd used her checking account to buy a one-way ticket to Guatemala, where he was from."

"Oh, no." Tessa couldn't imagine how he must have felt. Or what his mother had gone through. "So you got him?"

"Got him, booked him, now he's doing time. She wasn't his first victim, and when he gets out he probably won't be his last." He swung the truck onto the off-ramp. "I hate it that she nearly lost everything she'd worked for her whole life. But what I hate more is that she lost her faith in people. He stole part of my mom that won't come back, and that's what burns me the most."

He took a westbound street that would take them to the waterfront.

"I think she's lucky to have you," Tessa said. "You saved her from a lot of misery."

"Yeah, maybe."

Grouch he might be. Authority figure—yeah, that, too. But Tessa couldn't fault him for caring about his mom, as she did hers.

If nothing else, at least they had that in common.

8

THE BOUNCER at the door went by the name of Olie and looked like an ex-WWF wrestler or maybe a runaway extra from a Viking epic. He took the picture of Christina and studied it by the light over the nondescript door on which *Atlantis* was stenciled in black paint.

"Nope. Never seen her before. Brunettes are my thing. I'd have remembered her."

"How many guys does the club have on the door?" Griffin asked.

"Six of us. Two on weeknights, four on weekends, when the bar gets covered, too. Eight-hour shift and free drinks. Not a bad gig. I'm going to cooking school in the daytime so I needed an evening job."

Griffin wondered if he gave out this much personal information to everyone. No matter. It beat the hell out of a long, frustrating attempt at interrogation.

"Where's the other bouncer? I'd like to show this to him, too."

"John's probably inside."

They found John talking with the bartender, but like Olie, neither of them could remember seeing Christina before. And the manager was no help, either.

"Are you a cop?" he asked from behind the desk in an office that looked like the inside of an aluminum trash can, all smooth metallics and black-on-silver design. "Got a warrant?"

"No and no," Griffin said. What a jerk. Clearly, he didn't know it took more than a soul patch to make him cool. "I just need to talk to your weekend bouncers. I'm a private investigator working on a missing persons case."

"You'll have to come back Saturday, then," the manager said. "I ain't giving out the names and numbers of my people. That's confidential."

"A girl's life may be in danger," Tessa put in quietly. "We need to talk to them. Tonight, if possible."

"That ain't my lookout." He shook his head. "My people are my lookout. Come back Saturday."

He waved them out the door and that was that. Tessa glanced at Griffin as they walked down the stairs, but he was busy trying to control the urge to walk back in there and choke a few names out of the guy.

When they pushed open the doors, they saw the club had begun to fill up and the music and light show had reached titanic proportions. Tessa had to shout to make herself heard.

"Now what?"

"Fall back to Plan B," he said. "We'll cruise around and see what you can pick up."

The suede fringe on Tessa's skirt swung as she crossed the dance floor and began to make a slow circuit of the room. Griffin found his anxiety and frustration fading as he followed her. He had no idea what to expect. A trance, such as she'd gone into earlier? Some kind of information flow like that of a Geiger counter? That was too far out of his league. He was better at close observation, and as they pushed through the crowd, the music reverberating around them, he found himself unable to do anything else.

It was no hardship to observe Tessa and her curvy little rear end wrapped in soft suede. The fringe brushed against her thighs, parting and falling together again every time she took a step. It was hypnotic, almost. Parting and falling. Parting and falling.

What's the matter with you?

Just because it wasn't a hardship to look at her didn't mean she was suddenly interesting to him in a sexual way. Not at all.

Just because she seemed to know what she was doing and might actually be able to help him didn't mean they were in some kind of partnership. Wrong. He was a glorified babysitter. Or, as she'd said herself, a recording secretary.

He dragged his gaze off her legs and the fringe and fixed it on the back of her neck as he trailed behind her. There was no particular method in her movements. She'd pause by a table or a stool, wait for a moment, then move on and touch a mirror or a string of glass bubbles suspended in the air. There were no fake fishing nets and naked mermaids at the Atlantis. It was all about glass and transparency and the way light broke in wavy patterns on people's faces as they danced.

Flakes of light glimmered in Tessa's hair as she bent her head to consider the railing of a circular staircase that led to the loft, where there seemed to be a restaurant. The light moved like a sprinkling of fairy dust on the back of her neck, which was exposed by the blunt cut of her hair as it fell forward.

He'd never realized before how vulnerable a woman's nape was. How slender yet strong it looked. Maybe it was the contrast of soft skin against the hard transparency of the glass and the bubbles and the Lucite treads of the stairs. Or maybe it was just Tessa.

He and his bad attitude had hurt her feelings a dozen times since she'd arrived this afternoon. He'd bullied and blustered in the very best Singleton tradition, and she'd done nothing but straighten her spine and force him to focus on Christina. She'd held to her job description when he'd been busy resenting the fact that she'd even been given a job.

If they were going to be successful, he was going to have to start over with her somehow. If she'd let him.

He took a breath to say something along that line, when she turned. "I'm not getting anything," she said. "Sorry about that. I really thought I could."

"Don't worry about it." The music segued from a brisk salsa number into something he actually recognized. "Smooth," by Santana and Rob Thomas. "We can head out if you—"

But she was no longer listening to him. She'd whirled away onto the dance floor, her body pulsing as her feet moved with the salsa step. She lifted her arms above her head, giving herself up to the beat, her hips describing circles that only a guy made of solid rock wouldn't recognize as the movements of a woman in the throes of sex.

Two men materialized out of thin air to dance with her, and she turned to face them both, laughing.

So smooth. She'd said that earlier. Did the song have some kind of effect on her because of Christina? Did he care? No, what he cared about right now was getting her out of the grip of Nitwit Number 1, who seemed determined to pantomime orgasm with her plastered up against him.

He grabbed the guy by the arm and told him where to go.

"Take it easy, man," he said resentfully, brushing his sleeve back into place. "It's just a dance."

"Yeah, well, she's with me."

They faded into the crowd and there was Tessa, doing the shimmy right in front of him. "Dance with me."

"I think we should go."

"This is it," she said, and danced around him. "This is their song."

His brain had a split second to absorb the words before he found himself attempting to mimic her steps, something he generally avoided like wasps' nests and crack houses.

"Like this," Tessa said, and grabbed the waistband of his jeans on either side. "Move your feet like mine. One-two-three. One-two-three."

Was that all there was to it? Or was it the fact that she was plastered up against him and her thighs guided his in the beat while her breasts brushed his chest? His brain lost the ability to focus on anything else but Tessa's body and the sinuous way she moved, as though the music had wound itself inside her and was pulsing through her body and into his.

"This song was playing when they were here." She did a slow revolution with her arms raised and her suede-covered derriere brushed the front of his pants. Griffin swallowed and hoped no one could see his erection in the crowd.

"He made his decision while they danced," she said when she was facing him once more.

"What decision?"

"I don't know. Just a decision."

"And who is *he?*"

"Don't know that either. But someone mature. I thought before that her boyfriend isn't someone her age. He's definitely older."

"How much older?"

"It's hard to tell. Fifteen years, maybe? Twenty?"

"Good God."

"Someone old enough to know better, anyway. He could still be the kidnapper, but I'm beginning to doubt it."

Talking was good. Talking kept him from thinking about her body and what it was doing to his. "We've got to find him. We've got no choice but to come back here Saturday night and talk to the other bouncers."

"Anything could happen by Saturday night."

"Let's hope not."

"So what now?" She swayed gently against him in time with the music, her fingers again hooked in his belt loops. Griffin wasn't sure which would be worse—holding her this close or doing the professional thing and stepping away. He couldn't remember the last time he'd done something—like this, for instance—for the pure pleasure of it. But how could he step away from a woman who made his blood dance with the same dark, insistent beat as the music?

But he had a feeling that if a man got involved with Tessa Nichols, "normal" might be something he'd have to kiss goodbye for good.

No way was he getting involved. He dragged his mind off the woman and onto the question she'd asked. "We might as well head back. Unless you want to hang around and listen for more music, there's nothing else we can do here."

"We could dance." She grinned up at him and tugged on either side of his waistband, as if to show him how to swivel his hips.

He could show her some hip action, all right. It just wouldn't be here.

Or anywhere. She's not your kind of woman, Knox.

"Stay if you want," he said gruffly, to cover up the fact that his body would be only too happy to follow her teasing lead. "Take a cab home and Jay will pick up the tab. I'm heading out."

"All right, all right. It was just a suggestion." She followed him out of the club and down the street to where he'd parked the truck. The wind off the harbor crept under his jacket and chilled him. It had been damned hot in there. Hot music, hot atmosphere…and a very hot woman.

He had to stop this. Had to stop thinking of her in those terms.

Unlike the trip out, where she'd extracted more information than he'd revealed to anyone but the staff therapist at the Santa Rita P.D. after the shooting, Tessa was quiet on the trip home. He was almost afraid to start up a conversation in case she weaseled her way into his head again and started on some other forbidden topic, like his ex-wife. And then there was the damn skirt, with its fringe falling open on either side of her thighs and revealing about a mile of soft, bare skin and slender leg.

Griffin felt almost relieved as they turned into the driveway and approached the dark bulk of the house. He had to get out of the enclosed space of the cab before he did something he would regret, like reach out and touch her. He couldn't wait to get home, where everything was normal and no visions of Tessa would intrude.

The house wasn't as dark as he'd thought. "Looks like Jay's still up," he observed, turning off the engine and climbing out.

Jay was not only up, he was waiting for them. "Well?" He came out of his office as they crossed the entry hall. "What did you find out?"

"Not a lot," Griffin confessed. "The two guys on the door didn't recognize Christina's picture, and the other four won't come on duty until the weekend. We'll have to go back." He added, "The manager wouldn't give us their names or numbers, so we didn't have a lot of choice."

"Did you explain to him that this could be a matter of life and death?"

"Yes, without going into details that might pin down whose life we're talking about," Tessa said. "It didn't do any good. I did get a faint reading there, though. Enough to tell me that the person whose attention she was trying to get really is an older man. Maybe twenty years older."

"What?" Jay's face was a mix of horror and confusion. "Who?"

"We don't know yet," she said. "But give me time."

"We may not have time!"

"If you'd let me bring in the P.D. we might—" Griffin began, but Jay cut him off.

"I already said no. We'll do the best we can."

Griffin bit back an angry retort that would have included something about rope and tied hands. "I'm out of here, then," he said instead. "See you in the morning."

"What, already?" Jay glanced at his Rolex. "It's not even eleven."

"I'm sure Tessa could use some sleep," he said. "It's been a long day."

"I don't know about that." Tessa stretched like a cat and Griffin swallowed and looked away. "I'm still wired from dancing." She dropped her arms. "Hey, I know. Why don't you come out to the cottage and we'll go through her music collection. Music is obviously a big deal to her. I bet she's got Santana's *Supernatural* and if she does, maybe I get can something from it."

"Good idea." Jay sat behind the desk and settled in front of the computer as though he meant to work into the night. "Whatever the hell *Supernatural* is. It's appropriate, if you ask me."

Griffin closed his eyes briefly and resigned himself to yet more efforts at control. Tessa in a suede miniskirt. Tessa dancing. Now Tessa in the cottage alone with him, in the miniskirt, probably dancing.

Supernatural, for sure.

9

From the private journal of Jay Singleton

Okay. Still with the older man. What a theory. Much as this makes me sick, I also don't have to be a shrink to see what's going on.

Is my little girl really hitting on older guys as some kind of substitute for attention from me? When we find her, she's going into therapy. This has to be fixed. How in the hell could I have given her attention when I was on the other side of the country trying to make enough money to keep two households going? So I missed her eighth-grade graduation and her prom and some godawful father-daughter thing Barbara made a big stink about. Those were just events. Nothing affected the bedrock of my love for my little girl.

I did the best I could. Some guys make dramatic gestures, like whipping a prom dress out of a box. Some guys go and scream at soccer games and fight with other parents behind the fence. But what did I do? I just loved her. A man has to get credit for that, doesn't he? My gestures aren't very dramatic, but they kept her fed and clothed and in a good school, didn't they?

Is this some kind of punishment for not being around? The phone works both ways, you know. Not to mention the fact that a private-school education is damned expensive.

Why is nobody giving me credit for what I did do, instead of making me feel like shit for what I didn't do?

"I HOPE YOU didn't really want to go home," Tessa said as they crossed the patio. Lamps on posts at intervals around the flagstone square illuminated it gently.

Because of course he had a home. Somehow she'd pictured him spending his nights standing up outside Jay's office, like a deactivated droid. "Where do you live?"

"In Santa Rita. It's okay. We have a job to do. I can sleep anytime." Griffin opened the door to the cottage and stood aside so Tessa could pass him. "That said, I still think we'd get further faster if he'd call in the P.D. If something happens to Christina, he's not going to be able to live with it."

Tessa shivered. It was true. Singleton had cut off one hand of the investigation and without it they were nearly helpless.

The thought brought another chill. Or maybe it was just the fog moving in for the night, breathing in through the cottage's open windows. She crossed the room and closed them, turned on a lamp, then took her blue sweater out of the suitcase and tugged it on over her T-shirt.

Wearing something this clingy to a club was one thing, but after those circus remarks earlier, she figured he'd rather she were covered head to foot in baggy sweats. There were two reasons for that. One, he was attracted to her. Or two, he didn't like women.

She had a feeling it was definitely not option two. Not that it mattered to her one bit. She was not excited by a grumpy ex-cop, no matter how well he danced.

He is for damn sure excited by you. And is trying for all he's worth not to be, which is kind of insulting when you think about it.

He's an honorable man, she reminded herself. He wasn't going to jump her bones just because they were alone together late at night in these cozy surroundings. But she had felt the desire coming off him in waves, both at the club and in the truck on the way home. It was hot and dark and exciting, and she had no idea what to do about it.

Enjoy it, silly.

Right. Hey, they could go at it like minks in this room and then be all cool and Sherlock Holmes in the daytime.

She could. She doubted he could, though.

"Let's see what she's got in her CD rack." Tessa knelt next to the bookshelf, which, instead of holding books, held about a thousand CDs and DVDs for the compact entertainment center on that wall.

The truth was, once she'd gotten over the arrest thing—which had happened right around the time he'd admitted he had been wrong to do it—she'd found herself liking things about him. Riding to his mom's rescue. Keeping his temper instead of knocking the chip off the club manager's shoulder.

And—okay, deep, dark confession time here—she liked that he was attracted to her. Maybe that was why she'd chosen the suede skirt. Maybe she'd wanted to provoke a reaction—exactly the reaction, in fact, that he'd had. And perversely, she liked that he hadn't acted on it. It was strong. It was sexy. It was a challenge, and the only challenges she'd had lately were the kind that involved thesis topics. This was much more interesting.

Uh-huh. I thought you weren't into cops? "Scary whack jobs," I believe you call them.

Those are the ones Linn works with. They're probably honorable men, too, but you still wouldn't want to get involved with a guy who could go out and shoot someone as part of his job. Besides, Griffin isn't a cop anymore. He's just a guy who thinks I'm hot.

You are so pathetic. When did you say you had sex last?

"Uh…don't you want to change or something?" he said from behind her.

She glanced over her shoulder, surprised. "What, into something more comfortable?"

He shrugged. "It's just a suggestion. When I get home from work it's the first thing I do."

She stood and gave him a curious look. "Griffin, does the way I dress make you nervous?"

"No, not at all." He picked up the perfume bottle from the vanity, seemed to realize what it was a moment too late, and put it down. "You just said you needed a nurturing, comfortable environment to bring on a vision, that's all."

"And you're sure it has nothing to do with my skirt?"

He straightened his spine, as if he were on review and his commanding officer was inspecting his shoes. "Of course not."

Which meant, of course, that it did. Smothering a smile, she said, "You're probably right." She got up from the floor and pulled her peach flannel pajama bottoms and the tank top that went with them out of the suitcase. "Back in a sec."

In the bathroom, she kicked off her sandals and changed quickly, then pulled on the blue sweater again. Bouncing out there with nothing between them but a thin film of cotton jersey was probably not going to help him feel more comfortable around her, though she had no problems with it. He liked looking at her breasts, so what was wrong with letting him? She could comply with the letter of the law the way he was laying it down, but the way the sweater draped over her braless curves didn't exactly hide them.

Too bad. If he wanted her in sweats, he was going to have to say so. She wasn't going to make this easy for him. This was temporarily her bedroom, after all.

As she opened the door, she felt his gaze on her, as warm as the cashmere sweatshirt.

"Now then, where were we?" Just as she reached out to pick up a CD, the world wavered, as though a transparent curtain billowed in the space between reality and dream.

"Oh, my," she said. "It's a—"

And then reality went away.

"IT'S A WHAT?" Griffin watched her straighten, her gaze fixed on the middle distance. Her eyes moved from one point to another and back again, as if she were watching the action on a movie screen.

Watching. Of course.

The hair on the nape of his neck stood on end as he realized that for all intents and purposes, Tessa Nichols had left the building. The question was, where was she? And could she talk while she was there? She'd answered questions before, so maybe it would work here, too.

Griffin moved to stand next to her. "Where are you?" he asked softly.

"Don't know." Her voice came from far away, pitched just above a whisper.

"What can you see?"

"A window. With orange curtains. A motel sign. It flashes."

Griffin's heart sank. A motel meant Christina and her captor were on the move. Once they were on the road, it would be nearly impossible to track them down.

"Are you Christina?"

"No. She's there, lying on the bed."

"Tied up?"

"No." She paused. "Nice camisole. Silk, with thick lace trim. He's buying her things."

Of course he would. She'd left with nothing but her purse. But buying things meant credit card receipts, which meant a trail to follow. Too bad they didn't have a name to start with.

Buying things also probably meant they weren't dealing with a kidnapper at all. And buying high-end silk meant Tessa had been right about the older boyfriend.

Griffin didn't know whether to be relieved that Christina was probably not in the danger they'd feared, or furious that she and the boyfriend would put her family through this.

"She's smiling," Tessa whispered. "Looking up. He's in the bathroom doorway, next to the bed."

"Describe him."

"Tall. Dark hair. Dark eyes. He's looking at her like he's hungry."

"What's he wearing?" *Just give me a clue. Anything.*

"Nothing."

Okay. On to Plan B. "Any identifying marks or scars?" Griffin wondered how specific she could be.

"He's very well hung," she sighed, tilting her head to one side. "He looks at her like she's the only woman in the world."

As the kids said, T.M.I. He would have been quite happy not knowing *that.*

"Now he's lying down beside her. Touching her. He runs one finger under the strap of her camisole. She sits up and takes it off. It's brand-new. He's ripped her underwear off her before, but she doesn't want him to do that to this. It's too nice."

"Was it rape before?" The question was torn out of him. If so, how was he going to tell Jay?

"Oh, no," that faraway voice reassured him. "Not at all."

"Now what's happening?"

"He's touching her. Kissing her. Here." She lifted her hands and cupped her breasts, and Griffin nearly swallowed his tongue. All his sensible questions fled his brain like a startled flock of birds, replaced by the sight of Tessa, her head thrown back, cupping her breasts in both hands in exactly the way she had before, in this very room.

His jeans tightened with the suddenness of his erection. He'd give anything to be able to make some kind of noise and break this up, but then they might miss a valuable clue. Somehow he had to find the objectivity to tough it out. Maybe he could think about what he was going to charge this guy with when he found him. Or maybe—

Tessa stroked her hands down her ribs, to her hips, to her thighs, and his brain fritzed out again. "He's touching her all over. She's so in love, every touch is setting her on fire. She's impatient. Wants him to hurry."

Oh, God, was she going to watch them have sex and take him through it, play by play? "What color is the motel sign?" he blurted in desperation.

Tessa's eyes moved to the left, and her hands stopped on her pelvic bones in midcaress. "Black and yellow."

Griffin commanded his neurons to focus. The Super 8 motel chain had a black-and-yellow logo. That narrowed the field to, say, fifty possible places in three states that were within fourteen or fifteen hours' drive.

She moved, her back to him, and leaned into his chest. "He's spooning her. They're just so in love."

Her soft derriere, covered only by the thin cotton of the

pajama bottoms he'd practically forced her into putting on, snugged up against the erection that wouldn't go away despite his best efforts to change the subject. He should have stuck with the damn skirt. Griffin's breath hitched as she bent her knees a fraction of an inch, then straightened, her hips doing a sinuous figure eight with each rise and fall.

"Tessa," he said hoarsely.

Her eyes were half-closed. "She likes his arm around her. It makes her feel safe."

Reaching down, she took both his hands and cupped them on her breasts, holding them there with her own while she did that thing with her hips against his pelvis. His jeans threatened to explode. A sound halfway between a whimper and a moan came out of his throat, but he couldn't help it. Through the layers of cashmere and whatever stretchy thing she had on under it, the soft, round weight of her breasts filled his hands. Rigid nipples poked against his fingers. He'd been right, he thought through the red haze of desire. They were small and pointed and tight and there was nothing he wanted more in the world than to pull up her sweater and taste them. Right now.

"Yes," she sighed, and tipped her head back to nuzzle the side of his throat.

One more second, and he'd do something to bring her out of this. Just one sweet lift and a gentle squeeze of her soft flesh, one illicit moment of pleasure he would probably regret because clearly he was a coward and totally taking advantage of—

She gasped and jumped a little in his arms, then turned to look up into his face. Her startled expression melted into a smile that held a mix of humor and carnal knowledge. "Well, well," she purred. "Mr. Knox, did you change your mind?"

He stared at her for a moment while reality and dream collided, crashed, and fell into pieces around him. Tessa was back—and she was coming on to him. He released her and took a step back.

"I—we were…I mean, you were demonstrating what Christina was doing."

"Did you like it?"

"I—you were telling me, and then you took my hands and—" He never stammered. *Get a grip, Knox.* "We were replicating what you saw," he said firmly.

"Oh, I remember what I saw. Know what I see now?"

Oh yeah, he knew. The fact that she was looking at his crotch with undeniable interest was not helping.

Not one bit. He was as hard as a cop's baton and couldn't do a damn thing about it. "I'm sorry." The apology felt just as inadequate as it sounded. "I'm going now."

"Why? We were going to listen to music." She looked so touchable, while the lamplight glinted on her hair and traced the curves that had felt like heaven in his hands.

"Tomorrow," he got out, feeling for the door handle behind him. "Good night."

He broke the land speed record getting back to his truck.

10

MEN.

Tessa sank onto the end of the bed and shook her head, but whether at herself or at him, she could hardly tell. Nine guys out of ten would have grabbed an opportunity like that with both hands, so to speak. But no, she had to get the one honorable man in the bunch.

Or maybe it was simpler than that. Maybe he just wasn't into her, as the saying went.

Not true. He was totally into her in a sexual way. And she was certainly partial to a long-legged man with focus and smarts and the kind of mouth that made a woman think about sin. She was willing to overlook his less desirable traits, such as his habit of arresting people without evidence, or his lack of belief in people's talents, if he would just use that mouth on her.

Because this wasn't about white picket fences or whatever was bothering him. She was an adult, he was an adult, and to the best of her knowledge they were both free to act on their attraction.

Too bad he wasn't seeing it that way. Yet. Because it had been a long time since she'd felt such a rush of pleasure simply from being touched. Yes, okay, she'd been in the middle of a sensuous vision and had come out of it to find him reenacting it with her. That was a new one, she had to admit, and no wonder she was left humming like a live wire.

But it wasn't often that a man's hungry gaze could turn her on the way Griffin's did. Guys looked at her, sure, but most of the time it was an annoyance—as though she were improving the scenery for their benefit. Griffin looked at her as though she were unique, as though he was memorizing each curve as she revealed it to him.

You are feeling every one of the months since you last had sex, girl.

She was feeling something, that was for sure.

Tessa pulled off her sweater and lay back on Christina's coverlet, which was made of soft lavender velvet stitched all over in swirling patterns. The last time had been with Kent, the artist who had wanted her to model for him. She had no idea why she'd gone out with him in the first place. Artists were great, but after growing up with two of them, she tended to go for variety, such as a fellow grad student in the psych program, a software designer who had literally forgotten about her when he'd hit deadline on his project, and a guy who ran a bakery and kept really odd hours. She'd gained fifteen pounds dating him and had to work all of them off when they'd agreed to part. So when she'd met Kent at a party the psych student had thrown, she'd shrugged her shoulders and gone out with him. The problem was, he was so fixated on how she looked in connection with light, fabrics, even seating that she'd begun to get a little paranoid about it. He could care less what she thought, but how she looked meant everything to the guy. When he'd started choosing her lipstick colors "to give her skin tone a nice contrast," she'd called it quits.

Griffin didn't look at her like that—as if he were mentally framing a composition shot. Griffin looked at her the way a hungry man hurries by a bakery window, glancing over his shoulder to catch the last sight of the éclair. Wanting but not having.

She was going to have to invite him in, that was all. Let him know he could look and touch. And eat, too.

His hands had felt so good. She touched her breasts, holding them the way he had held them, but her hands were smaller and didn't have that sense of gentle urgency. He had touched her nipples, too, the briefest of caresses, but still, they had leaped to attention under his fingers. She brushed them with her own. Yes, it had felt like that. She wished he would use his thumb and forefinger to roll them, like this, giving her a taste of what his mouth might be like.

She imagined how good his tongue would feel, and his teeth, too, nibbling her nipples and sucking. Her fingers mimicked the motion and she felt an answering throb of need deep inside. He would spend a lot of time pleasuring her breasts—at least as much time as he'd spent looking at them lately.

What would he do if she slipped into a tank top and conveniently forgot to wear a bra? He'd probably have a coronary. Or at least an orgasm.

She smiled at the thought.

This was good. Say she wore the tank top. Say he couldn't take his eyes off her. Say he'd be sitting at a table and she'd come up and bend over to tell him something. Ooh, what would he do then? Jump up and run away? Or bury his face in her cleavage? Knowing Griffin, probably neither. But he would look. Oh, how he would look, the way he had this afternoon, mentally taking her clothes off and making love to every inch of her.

That was what she liked about his gaze. No, wanted. She wanted his gaze on her—on her mouth, on her breasts, on her ass and legs. Her hands moved down her body, as though Griffin's gaze were a physical thing.

It was, really. She could practically feel it, as hot and tactile as his hands.

A tiny rush of creamy fluid escaped her at the thought. He wasn't even here and the thought of him turned her on unbearably. She wanted him to touch her. She wanted his mouth on her breasts and between her legs. She wanted his tongue to flick and taste and suck and bring her ecstasy. She wanted that thick erection he couldn't hide in her hands. Then inside her body. She wanted to impale herself on him.

Tessa groaned, and slipped one hand under the elastic waistband of her pajama bottoms. With the other, she teased her nipples, imagining Griffin's tongue swirling on them. Her finger slipped between her vulva and found a pool of fluid waiting for him to taste.

Oh yes, his tongue there, too. Her clit practically wept with welcome at the thought. His strokes would be long, like this, teasing, oh, he could eat her while she fondled her breasts with both hands and he watched, oh yes, he'd like that.

He'd eat her, yes, that tongue, stroking faster and faster, while his cock hardened and thickened and threatened to burst with desire—

"Take me!" she cried, and her orgasm exploded under her frantic fingers, shaking her body, making her break out in a sweat, leaving her breathless on the coverlet in the golden lamplight as she shuddered in the aftermath of pleasure.

If only he could see her now, plunge into her after he'd brought her to such a release. If only he could lose himself in her, explode into orgasm too, and ride the wave of desire to its crashing end.

If only he could be with her.

If only she weren't alone.

IF HE COULD JUST control his body, he wouldn't have to live through this kind of humiliation.

Griffin let himself into the house and flipped on the nearest light switch. Had it only been this morning that he'd broken the coffee carafe? The air in the house was faintly scented with it, a reminder of a time when he'd been relatively in control of his life.

Before Jay had called.

Before Tessa.

He toed off his boots and padded down the hall to the bathroom, where he stripped and stepped into the shower. He'd needed a cold one a half hour ago. Now all that was left of his hard-on was a simmering frustration and some stiffness in his bum knee where he'd twisted it tripping over her suitcase. He'd have to put ice on it tonight or it would twinge every time he turned around tomorrow.

It was one thing to deal with the consequences of his injury. It was quite another to deal with the consequences of touching Tessa.

He dried off vigorously and pulled on a pair of sweats. In the kitchen, he pulled a cold pack out of the freezer and a beer out of the fridge, then settled onto the couch to nurse both knee and beer and figure out how he was going to handle this.

Because it had to be handled, this attraction between them. He hadn't managed to survive six years of being single by losing it or running away every time a woman came on to him. Oh, he could enjoy sex, no problem. He liked women—liked looking at them, liked being around them, liked talking with them and having the occasional good laugh. But as for letting a woman grab control of his heart and emotions, just to strangle him with them—that was not going to happen again.

It had only been in the last year or so that he'd been able to look at his relationship with the woman responsible for this philosophy—his ex-wife—with any kind of objectivity, without that sick wave of grief and betrayal ambushing him. He had even found a certain measure of peace in the fact that Sheryl was happy, even if it was with Caleb Morgan and not him.

The simple fact was that he had failed to keep his marriage alive, the same way he had failed to see the kid with the gun in that darkened hallway. One had broken his heart and the other his body.

After that, who could blame him for having a healthy sense of self-preservation?

The phone on the end table next to his elbow rang, making him jump. He grabbed for the ice pack and settled it on his knee while he glanced at the clock. Late-night calls, in his experience, usually didn't contain good news.

"Knox."

"Hey, bro. Don't you ever check your messages?"

Griffin cocked an eye at the digital display on the phone console. Four messages. "I just got home. What's wrong?"

"Nearly midnight and you just got home?" Rhys sounded incredulous. "I heard that Jay Singleton was a slave driver and this proves it."

"Not all of us have cushy programming jobs. Are you going to tell me what's up or not?"

"Just wanted to let you know that you're a proud uncle of a little girl, that's all. Jess went into labor yesterday."

"Geez. How come nobody called me?"

"Uh, rewind to original question about the messages."

"I have a cell phone," Griffin reminded his brother. "It's good for times like this. So are baby and mom okay?"

"Healthy and tired and completely okay. Dad is a wreck and Tyler's not sure about this girl business, but he'll come around."

"Congratulations, Rhys. I'll come up and see you guys as soon as I can. What about Mom—is she there?"

"We wouldn't be functioning if she wasn't. She came up to Petaluma at the beginning of the week. She and Tyler have been having a great time. Plus I think I gained five pounds. I forgot how good her macaroni casserole is. So, what's going on that you're working eighteen-hour days?"

"Oh, the usual. Some internal stuff came up. Very hush-hush. Jay wanted me on it personally."

"Uh-huh. You know, if you keep making his life easy you're never going to have one of your own."

Griffin snorted. "I have a life."

"You have a case of social atrophy you're calling a life."

"Geez, you sound like Tessa." Then he winced and resisted the sudden urge to smack himself on the forehead. Stupid, stupid, stupid!

"Tessa? Who's Tessa? My God, is there actually someone lurking on the fringes of your sorry existence? A female someone?"

"It's nothing."

"Nothing, huh? But I'm sounding like her. This means actual conversation has occurred. Spill, bro. Who is she?"

"Just someone I'm working with."

"What kind of a someone? Blond, brunette, redhead? Beautiful, smart, solvent?"

"Blond, beautiful, smart, and an economic disaster. But on the plus side, she drives a '66 Mustang ragtop."

"My God." Rhys sounded as if he was about to have an orgasm. "You have to bring her when you come up. No arguments."

"I don't know if things will progress to the meet-the-family stage. It's just physical. And we're working together, so even that's out of bounds."

"Bull." Rhys's scorn indicated ethics like that deserved to go the way of the dodo bird. "We need that car in the family. Don't disappoint me."

"Okay for you. You're not the one going crazy."

"If you're going crazy, that means you're over Sheryl. For which you'll observe me on my knees thanking God."

"Yeah, me, too. But I don't know. Tessa's—different."

"Different how? Different like she isn't a boring cop type, or different like she just got released from Vacaville?" he asked, naming northern California's correctional and psychiatric institution.

How was he going to explain this? "She's a sensitive. As in, she uses psychometry to find things or people."

A long silence hissed down the line.

"Rhys?"

"I'm still here. My mind tried to wrap itself around that and started unraveling instead."

"You really sound like her. Too bad you're already married."

His little brother, he of the genius IQ and the runaway mouth, ignored him. "And Jay has you working on something with her. And she's beautiful and driving you crazy. I dunno, bro. Sounds like you're on your own with this one."

"Yeah, I know."

Being on his own with Tessa was the whole problem.

11

WHEN TESSA WOKE, the sun was streaming through the window next to the door in brilliant squares, so she did a few yoga stretches in their warmth to start things off and put herself in a positive frame of mind.

She hadn't dreamed about Christina, as she'd hoped when she'd shut off the light and gone to sleep in the girl's bed. Instead, she'd dreamed about making love with Griffin—gee, what a surprise. He'd been just as delicious in her dream as he had been in her fantasy…and just as gone when she woke up.

Ah well, one had to take the bad with the good in this life, she thought philosophically as she walked over to the main house, let herself in through the kitchen door and went in search of coffee and food.

Jay was lying in wait in his office like one of those jumping spiders, and he popped out of his doorway as she crossed the foyer.

"Tessa. Can we talk?"

"Good morning to you, too," she said.

"Oh. Good morning. In here." He ushered her into the office and she spared a moment to wonder if he ever left it. Then she decided he must. He was wearing a different colored shirt.

Griffin was standing in his usual spot by the window

and there they were in that annoying power triangle again. Tessa was just about to do something outrageous, like push a pile of paper out of the way and sit on the edge of the desk, when Jay indicated the chair she'd commandeered yesterday.

"Have a seat. Coffee?"

You're making progress, girl. "Thank you." She sat in the wing chair and pulled her feet up under the gauzy purple skirts of her sundress, and Jay poured her a cup of coffee from the pot on the sideboard.

"Griffin says you saw something last night. Care to brief me?"

Calmly and in as much detail as she could, she told him everything she could remember. When she got to the part that involved Griffin's hands and body and what they'd been doing to her dreams all night, she stopped and took a fortifying sip of hot coffee. A quick glance in his direction told her he wasn't about to clue in his boss on that part, either. He straightened and looked at nothing in particular on the other side of the room.

"Griffin says the sign is probably the Super 8 logo," she finished.

"Which narrows the field to about fifty places within a day's drive of here," Griffin added helpfully.

"So you two think it's not a kidnapping?" Jay rubbed his eyes.

Okay, so maybe he wasn't sleeping in his office, but it was clear he wasn't sleeping much anywhere else. This had to be hell on him. She resisted the urge to reassure him that they were doing the best they could. No point belaboring the obvious.

"We've had no ransom demand and it's been twenty-four hours," Griffin said. "And Tessa's information seems to indicate there's an older man she's infatuated with, to the point that she has been trying to get his attention for some time. Now that she's succeeded, they seem to have gone somewhere for a tryst, or…something."

"It's the 'or something' that concerns me." Jay's voice was grim. "No matter how old he is, he's got the maturity of a thirteen-year-old if he doesn't make some effort to let us know where she is and that she's okay."

"Which is why we're going to stay with them," Tessa put in. "And then you can go and bring her back."

"Kicking and screaming, if necessary," he agreed. "So, what's our next move? Sit around and wait until the universe sends you another sign?"

"No," Griffin said dryly before she could answer. "Since we've agreed it may not be a kidnapping, we change our plan of attack. Does Christina have her cell phone with her?"

"As far as I know. We've called it about every hour, but she's got it turned off. It goes straight to voice mail."

"I need to see the bill. If she's been calling him, we can find out who he is."

"All her bills come to me." Jay hunted through one of the piles. "Here's one. How recent is it?"

Griffin tore it open and scanned it. "Damn it. It's the right month, but there are no call records. What's with that?"

"She probably gets them online," Tessa said. "That's how I do mine. It saves pages of trees that way." She smiled at them.

"Where's her laptop?" Griffin asked.

"In the cottage." Jay waved a hand at his electronic command center. "But why not use mine?"

Griffin shook his head. "If she's logging on to the phone

company's site, the cookies identifying her will be on her laptop."

Tessa snagged a muffin off the sideboard and followed Griffin outside, coffee mug in hand. "Even if you do find her records, how are you going to figure out which one might belong to this guy?"

"Process of elimination, to start. Then I call in a few favors."

"With whom?" They crossed the patio to the cottage.

"I still know a few people downtown."

"Or I could just call my sister. She's hooked into every system known to man."

With his hand on the doorknob, he glanced back at her. "Good," he said briefly. "We'll do that."

She blinked. Wow. She'd actually said something investigatorlike, something that had been accepted at face value. No sarcasm, no dismissal, and no begging someone to listen to her.

How about that.

The laptop was sitting in a shelving rack in the walk-in closet. Griffin plugged it in and booted it up. Then he stopped.

"What's the matter?"

He waved at the screen. "She's got the damn thing password protected. I can't even get to the desktop."

"Can't you—I don't know—hack into it or something?"

He shot her a look. "Can't you lay hands on it and get a vision?"

Uh, okay. Point taken.

Tessa gazed around the room. What did people use for passwords? Family names, nicknames, nouns, verbs, names of animals, names of pets—

"What's the elephant's name?" she said suddenly, zeroing in on the stuffed elephant she'd taken from between the pillows and put on the nightstand.

"Huh?" Griffin glared at the laptop as if it would yield the password simply by process of intimidation.

"The elephant she had on her bed. What's its name?"

"How should I know?" He flipped out his cell phone and pressed two buttons. *Fleedeep.*

"Yeah?" Jay's tinny voice responded.

"What's Christina's elephant's name?"

"What elephant?" Jay sounded completely lost.

"Here, give me that," Mandy's voice said in the background. "Griffin?"

"Still here."

"I don't know, either. You mean that stuffed toy on her bed, right?"

"Right. Who would know?"

"What about Lucia?" Tessa asked.

"Who?" Jay said in the background.

"Lucia," Mandy said. "My domestic assistant."

Was that what they were calling housekeepers these days? There was a scuffle as Mandy went to get Lucia, and then the girl herself came on the walkie-talkie.

"The elephant's name is Cleo, Señor Knox," she said.

"Hang on." Griffin typed the name into the password field and in a second the desktop opened up in all its glory. "Bingo. Thanks, Lucia." He shut the cell phone and put it back in his pocket. "Now, then," he said to the laptop, "spill."

Christina evidently put a lot of faith in her system password. Once they logged on, she had everything set up to open automatically, including the phone company's site.

"Holy cats." Tessa looked at the screen over his shoulder. "How many calls can one teenager make?"

The scent of his cologne intensified, as though his body temperature had risen. He might be trying to maintain his businesslike demeanor, but she knew how men's bodies worked.

"If Daddy's paying the bill, the sky's the limit." He shifted uneasily, and she took pity on him and straightened. He cleared his throat. "There are a lot of repeats, though. Grab a pen and write these down."

As it turned out, only thirteen numbers made up the four screens' worth of calls. Griffin ruled out the Boston exchanges right away, as well as the Pebble Beach Golf and Country Club.

"It's these ones in the local area codes that are interesting," he said, pointing to the last half a dozen on her sheet of note paper. "Let's see what we come up with."

Her sister, Linn, had told her about the part of her job that involved making undercover calls. Obviously this was a skill they learned in the academy, because during the next ten minutes, Griffin played the part of a surfer, an Ivy League freshman, and a bookstore clerk as he called one number after another. Four of them were Christina's girlfriends. One was the admissions office at UC Santa Rita. "Dad will be glad to hear about that," Tessa murmured. The last two numbers rang through to automated voice-mail systems with no personalized message.

"Interesting." Griffin closed his cell phone and indicated the two numbers. "Can you give those to your sister and ask her to do a subscriber check?"

Tessa wrote *subscriber check* in careful script on the paper and nodded. "We just might get lucky."

He shut down the laptop, but made no move to go. Instead, he slewed around on the edge of the bed and put the laptop aside. "Look, Tessa, I want to apologize for last night."

Apologize? After triggering all those lovely dreams? "I hate when guys say that," she said.

"I want to make it clear that I was following instructions I believed you were giving me while you were having the vision." He paused. "It's also clear that I enjoyed it a little too much. I took advantage of you and I'm sorry. It won't happen again."

There was nothing quite as annoying as having a man say he enjoyed it but it would never happen again. He might be able to say the words, but his body told her differently. Why fight it? She had to make some effort to turn his thinking around. A little mutual pleasure wasn't something to apologize for. It was something to appreciate. She just didn't think he saw it that way. "Accepted," she said.

A silence fell, as if he expected her to say more, and she heard the gulls calling over the boom of the breakers in the distance. And the more subtle, internal call of woman to man.

Then he asked, "So, how much awareness of the real world do you have when you see…things?"

He sounded as if he honestly wanted to know. You had to respect a guy who could admit he didn't know everything. Maybe the sun pouring through the cottage's windows was what had inspired this moment of clarity.

"I kind of lose track of my body."

His eyes traced her from neckline to sandals, and it happened again—that feeling of heat, as if his gaze had laid a physical hand on her body. Her nipples tightened under the thin bodice of her dress.

And he saw her reaction. He swallowed again.

The poor guy was trying to have a sensible conversation. Maybe he wasn't as interested as she in the invisible give-and-take of attraction. Or maybe he was just better at blocking it out. She hadn't really verbalized what happened when she saw things to anyone before. Most people got weirded out or didn't care.

"My consciousness is so much in the world of the vision that there aren't any cycles left to spend on where my body is or what it's doing." She looked at him while he tried not to look at her. "I haven't come on to anyone before, though."

It seemed to be very important that he get the laptop closed properly because he pulled it onto his lap. "That's okay. Happens to me all the time."

She grinned. "I bet. You've totally got that Viggo Mortensen wounded-warrior thing going."

He looked up, his face a little blank. "What?"

"Never mind. So what did I do?" As if she didn't know. But sometimes if a guy had a hang-up about something, it was better to talk about it.

"You kind of backed into me and then took my hands and, um…"

"Put them on my breasts."

"Uh, yeah." He bit his lower lip.

Is there something there you want to hide? she thought wickedly. "And you enjoyed it."

"Yeah. Like I said, I'm sorry."

"Why is that something to be sorry for? I wasn't sorry."

She thought he might follow up on that, but he didn't. "I'm sorry I touched you without your permission." He glanced up. "Your conscious permission, that is."

"But my unconscious was all systems go. I would say that ought to tell us something."

"Like what?"

She was about to tell him exactly what, with maybe a

demonstration or two, but something held her back. Maybe it was the expression in his eyes—as if a deep, dark chasm had opened up at his feet.

"Like my unconscious needs to see a shrink," she said instead, smiling as though it was a joke and giving him an easy way out.

He took it without hesitation and got up. "Getting back to reality, we have a job to do. Let's concentrate on that."

"Sure. Whatever you say," she said, noticing with some disappointment that he no longer needed the laptop to shield himself from his reaction to her.

"I'll go update Jay."

"And I'll call my sister."

And weren't they just being all civil and totally avoiding what both of them wanted, which was to throw each other down on the lavender velvet bedspread and kiss each other into oblivion.

Tessa sighed, took a bite out of her muffin and a sip from the cold coffee, and reached for the phone on the nightstand.

GRIFFIN BERATED HIMSELF for getting into that conversation all the way into the house. What had he been thinking, telling Tessa Nichols he liked touching her when he had no intention of following up? That moment of honesty could have become downright dangerous.

He had neither the time nor the inclination to start something he couldn't finish, and even if he did, it wouldn't be with a blond psychic who represented everything he mistrusted. Besides, she only found him attractive when she wasn't really herself.

If that wasn't a kick to the manhood, he didn't know what was.

But why mistrust her? She's proving to be an asset.

He couldn't get past it. He needed facts. Evidence. Things that were real. She lived in some parallel universe half the time.

A parallel universe where she wants you, buddy. Think about it.

And just how weird was that?

12

"CLEU, THIS IS NICHOLS."

"Hi, it's me."

"Tessa?" Linn's tone went from hard-nosed cop to concerned sister. "Why are you calling me at work? Is something wrong?"

"No, not at all. In fact, you'll be happy to know I've got a paying gig. Remember that kidnapped girl I told you about?"

"The one you say you saw in some kind of vision?"

"Yeah. Turns out she wasn't kidnapped at all. We think she's run off with her boyfriend, and my gig is to find her. A missing persons deal."

"Why bother? I can sympathize. I'd like to run off with my boyfriend right now."

"She's only eighteen, and he's an older man. Daddy is very upset."

"Oh. Yeah, I could see that." Linn paused. "So what's up?"

"If I give you a couple of phone numbers, can you run them and find out who they belong to?"

"Phone numbers?"

"Yeah. Griffin says to ask you to do a subscriber check."

"Griffin? I only know one Griffin, and that's the one who arrested you two years ago and made me raise my

voice and say bad words in public. I didn't know you were
within a hundred miles of him."

"He works for the guy who hired me. Kind of a security guy."

"You sound awfully cheery for a woman working with
her arresting officer," Linn observed. "Especially when I
know you've been carrying around a lot of anger over it."

"The operative words being *over it.* I'm cool. He admitted he was wrong—well, sort of—and we've moved on."

"Griffin Knox admitted he was wrong. To a person he
arrested," Linn repeated the words flatly. "I never knew
that man to admit he was wrong about anything, and I
worked on the same squad with him for two years."

"I guess he's loosened up a bit." *He gets a hard-on
when he looks at me. That's definitely what I'd call loos-
ening up.*

No, no. You just didn't say things like that to Linn.

"So if I give you these numbers, can you help?"

"Sure. I guess. Strictly off the record, of course." Tessa
dictated them and Linn said, "I'll call you back in five minutes."

She was as good as her word. Tessa's cell phone beeped
a couple of notes of "Girls Just Wanna Have Fun" a few
minutes later, and when she answered it, Linn said, "I
don't know how much good this is going to do you."

"Why? Who do they belong to?"

"The first is assigned to someone called Michelle Oraia
at Oraia Salon, on First Street in Santa Rita."

"Hey, I know that place," Tessa said. "Or know *of* it.
Very exclusive. They definitely don't cater to the working
woman."

"The second is registered to a company called Stellar
Memory in Carmel Valley." She dictated both addresses

and Tessa wrote them down. The second one meant nothing to her, but hopefully it would ring a bell for Griffin.

"Thanks, Linn," she said. "I really appreciate this."

"No problem. It's not like you ask me for favors every day of the week. So, um…" She stopped.

"What?" It was very unlike Linn not to finish a sentence. "Did you find a florist?"

"Huh? Oh, yes, I did. Kellan's mom is going to do all the flowers. I don't know why I didn't ask her in the first place. No, I just wondered what it was like working with Griffin. If, you know, you're okay with it."

"I'm getting paid sixty bucks an hour to be okay with it. But no, I meant it. We're cool. We had a talk."

"Another revelation. There's a reason we called that guy Fort Knox, you know."

"I don't doubt it. He had a hard time with my, um, shall we say, investigative methods at first. But he's coming around now, since they seem to be providing information."

"Coming around how?"

Should she tell her? Oh, what the heck. "I kinda came on to him while I was having a vision. He's been apologizing ever since for responding. It's really annoying."

Tessa could practically feel Linn trying to revise her initial reaction, which was complete disbelief. "How can you come on to someone while you're seeing things?"

"It's hard to explain. It's like I'm describing what I see and acting it at the same time."

"And you do this in front of people?"

"Just him. His assignment is to report everything I say." She paused. "Well, almost everything."

"It's a good thing you're my sister. If it were anyone else I'd say they were bullshitting me," Linn said. "This is not the Griffin Knox I know. His wife dumped him when he was shot. Took off with his partner. Natalie Wong, my friend in Forensics, knows the whole story because she worked with his wife. Anyway, after that we started calling him Fort Knox, because no woman could crack him."

"People change. Not that it matters to me personally. He's not my type."

"I know. You're saving yourself for Coop or Danny."

"Don't even go there. Maybe I'll seduce Griffin just to prove you wrong."

"I don't think it's possible."

"What, that I could seduce someone?"

"Oh, I have every confidence in your ability to put a hex on some defenseless man and make him do your bidding. I just don't think that stuff works with Griffin Knox."

You didn't see his eyes when he looks at me. "Very funny. Thanks for the phone numbers."

"Anytime. Keep me posted."

Tessa hoped she was talking about the investigation, and not about the man.

UNFORTUNATELY, the subscribers to the phone numbers meant nothing to Griffin, either.

"A salon, okay, I can see her calling that repeatedly. But Stellar Memory? They manufacture computer parts. It must be a mistake."

"Or our mystery man works there." Tessa sat on the end of the bed, and leaned back with her elbows on the bedspread. The cottage had become command central with the addition of a Mission-style oak table provided by Mandy so they would have somewhere to put the laptop. A couple of yellow legal pads, some pens, and Griffin's cell phone sat on its glossy surface.

"Which narrows the field to what? A couple of hundred

people?" Griffin's tone was gloomy. "I could go over there and start asking questions, which would probably make other people ask questions, which would mean the media asking questions. I just don't see how we can pin down one guy on the quiet."

"Why so many calls to Oraia, though?" Tessa wondered aloud. "It's supposed to be really exclusive. You know, caters to the tennis-and-Jag set. But still, you call, you make an appointment, you wait two weeks to get in. You don't phone a bazillion times."

"Maybe she couldn't get the nail person she wanted."

"Was that a sarcastic remark?"

He glanced at her. "That girl isn't Jay's daughter for nothing. I wouldn't put it past her to nag until she got what she wanted."

"Hmm." Tessa wasn't satisfied.

"You can call over there and ask everyone in the place why Tessa called so often, if you want." From his tone, it was a dead end. "This Michelle Oraia is probably just a girlfriend and they're yakking, like she does with—" he held up the sheets of phone numbers "—Ashley, Melissa, and Georgia."

"You know what? I think I will. Something about this is bugging me."

He shrugged. "Suit yourself."

She dialed the salon's number and someone picked it up on the second ring. "Good morning, Oraia."

"Hi, can I speak to Michelle, please?"

"This is she. Can I help you?"

"Oh, I hope so." Tessa made her voice light and guileless. "Does Christina Singleton have an appointment there this week?"

The woman paused, and Tessa heard a page being

turned. "She does, as a matter of fact. Tomorrow at two, for henna and a trim."

"Um, just between you and me, do you think she'll make it?"

"Are you a friend of hers?"

"Yes, this is Ashley. I was thinking, you know, since she might not be back in town, you might let me have her appointment."

"So she actually did it, did she?" The young woman's voice lost its formality and took on a confidential tone. "To tell you the truth, I didn't think she'd go."

"I didn't, either. Not with her dad being so protective and all."

There was a pause. "You're way too nice. The guy's a total tyrant, making her check in every time she goes anywhere, always wanting to know where she is. This whole Trey thing was a major reaction to all that."

Trey?

Inside her, it felt as if a bell had rung, deep and sure. That was his name. Trey. The guy they were looking for.

"Do you know him very well?"

"No better than you. As much as you can know someone you only see in clubs and stuff. I mean, he talked as much to you as he did to her, which if you don't mind me saying, totally made Christina mad at you."

"Well, what was I supposed to do? Ignore my friend's guy? But I still don't know where they—"

"Oops, it's time to open up, and I promised I'd stay away. Why don't we wait and see if she calls, okay? If not, someone will let you know about that appointment tomorrow morning."

"Sure, that'd be fine."

Tessa said goodbye and hung up, grinning. She may not

have been able to ask where they were going, but at least she had a name. Damn, she was good at this investigative stuff.

She just hoped Ashley was in the mood for henna and a trim.

"WELL?"

The suspense was killing him.

Tessa practically glowed, she was so elated by her success with Michelle Oraia. Tessa glowing was a new one on him, Griffin thought. It would be safer and easier on his self-control if she wouldn't do that. Her eyes sparkled and her lips were parted, as if they couldn't wait to tell him the news.

He dragged his gaze off the lips and back to the eyes— the lesser of the two evils.

"This Michelle seems to be another of Christina's friends. She said that Christina took off for a tryst with a guy named Trey."

He flipped through the case files on the top level of the filing cabinet in his brain and came up blank. "Did you get a last name?"

She shook her head. "I think Ashley would have been expected to know, so I didn't ask. So totally cool, huh? Now we have something to go on."

"What made you decide to impersonate Ashley?"

"I just had a feeling. And it paid off." She sat on the bench and hugged her knees, the picture of delighted satisfaction.

"A feeling." With Tessa, that could mean anything. "Did you hear her thinking or something?"

"Of course not." Tessa crinkled her eyebrows in what he supposed was a frown. "It's like when the phone rings, you know? And you just know it's your mom, like you have a flash, or a word appears in your mind."

He was not going to touch that one. Flashes and words didn't generally appear in *his* mind. Give him something solid, like a spatter pattern or a fingerprint.

"So now what?" Tessa asked.

He walked over to the computer. "How about I see if there's a Trey anywhere at Stellar Memory?"

She came to stand behind his shoulder as he typed the name into the search function at the company's Web site. While he waited for the page to load, her scent tickled his nostrils. Jasmine and cotton and soap. The skin on his back tingled and his body tightened as his memory returned to this morning, when he'd looked at her and her nipples had—

"Wow, look at all those hits," she said, leaning closer.

Griffin blinked and came back to reality as the entries scrolled down the page.

Trey Ludovic, Chief Operating Officer, announced today...

Stellar Memory's Trey Ludovic said in a statement that...

COO places tenth in Bay to Berries run...

Griffin clicked on the last one. *Show me a picture,* he commanded the screen. There was a good chance that a community events article would have a photograph.

"Hey," Tessa said in surprise. "Wait a minute." She dashed out of the room.

Griffin stared at the door and then shrugged, returning his attention to the screen as the photograph finished loading.

And there he was. "Trey Ludovic, 41, of Stellar Memory crosses finish line to take tenth place." The guy was in damn fine shape for forty-one. Lean, muscular, his thick brown hair windblown, he grinned at the camera and even after a 10K run, looked ready to charm the Nikes right off the photographer.

"Look at this." Tessa handed him a framed photo and he recognized the group shot of the Christmas party that hung in the hallway. She pointed to someone in the back row, wearing a toga that managed to reveal way too much chest for a social occasion. "It's the same guy."

She was good. No doubt about it.

Griffin told the laptop to print the race article over their wireless network to the color printer in Jay's office.

"Come on. I'll bet you a beer Christina met him at the Christmas party, right here in the house."

Tessa followed him across the patio. "You realize that if it's someone he knows, Jay is totally going to blow a gasket and shoot something. Maybe us."

That was the risk you took when you worked for Jay Singleton.

13

"Christina ran away with Trey Ludovic?"

Tessa distinctly felt the glass in the windows rattle with the force of Jay Singleton's rage.

"I'll kill that two-faced S.O.B.!" he shouted. "I'll sell my stock—no, I'll buy his damn company and fire him. I'll make sure he never gets another job in the industry. And when he's homeless, I'll hunt him down with an elephant gun and he will be sorry—" he slammed a fist on the desk "—that he ever—" *Slam!* "—even *looked*—" *Slam!* "—at my daughter!"

Tessa eyed Griffin, waiting for a sign in case they were to run—or maybe perform CPR. Geesh. The guy had no medium setting. He was either enraged or Mr. Control Freak, with nothing in between. She wondered if he made love with his teeth clenched. Poor Mandy.

As if the thought had conjured her up—though it was probably the shouting—Mandy Singleton slipped into the room. She was wearing a multicolored wrap top that Tessa bet carried a Rodeo Drive label, and hot pink capri pants. It wasn't even lunchtime and she looked glossy and perfectly put together.

"Did you find something?" Mandy crossed the room and laid a hand on her husband's shoulder. "Jay, what's the matter?"

Jay told her, which made him erupt all over again. When the volcano had settled down to just a few spurts of lava spitting out now and again, Griffin spoke up. "Do you think it's possible they met at the Christmas party this past winter?"

"What the hell difference does it make where they met?" Singleton snapped. "The point is, where are they now?"

"The length of their relationship makes a lot of difference," Mandy said thoughtfully. "If she met him at Christmas and pursued him for, say, a couple of months before they began an affair, it could be fairly new. In that case it will be easier to break up. If they've been a couple for a year or more—"

"—they could be in Vegas getting married," Griffin finished.

That was not helpful. Tessa flashed him a glare.

Instead of punching out a window or throwing something, Singleton sat heavily in his upholstered chair and put his head in his hands. Mandy leaned down to hug him.

"That would be the worst-case scenario," Griffin added, evidently trying to soothe the poor guy's feelings. "Hopefully we can find her before that happens."

Jay was silent for a moment, then lifted his head. "As far as I know, she'd never met him before the Christmas party. She was living in Boston then, and flew out for it. I only got her to come out here to live in April."

Griffin looked at Tessa. "E-mail," he said.

She nodded. "We got so involved in the phone records, we forgot to check it."

"You think they might have been having an online affair between Christmas and April?" Mandy looked a little creeped out by the thought. Which was odd. After all, who was married to a much older man?

"We'll find out," Griffin said.

"But her physical pursuit of him didn't start until she got here," Tessa said. "I'm sure of that. Her clothes and things definitely give me that impression—longing, frustration, seduction." Jay flinched. "Sorry. But we have to deal with the truth, here."

"Why don't I see if I can track him down through his office?" Mandy suggested. "I can say I want to talk to him about a stockholders' barbecue or something. You know, part business, part personal. That will get past any executive assistant on the planet."

Tessa gazed at her in admiration. "You're good."

Mandy shrugged modestly. "It worked with Jay, didn't it?"

It must have.

"We'll see if we can find anything in her e-mail," Griffin said.

"And after that I'd like to go down to the beach." Tessa gazed out the window at the long line of breakers crashing in the distance. "Something about the beach is pinging on me."

"When she pings, you better listen," Jay advised, his voice a little muffled. His head was again in his hands.

"Understood." Griffin motioned toward the door, and Tessa preceded him back to their "office" in the cottage.

"Are we going to be able to get into her e-mail?"

Griffin leaned over the laptop and tapped a few keys. "If she's consistent, her mailbox should open right up when I—aha."

Tessa smothered a smile. And here she'd thought only detectives in books said "Aha."

Griffin paged through screens of messages, then started in on storage folders.

"Does it occur to you that we are grossly violating this girl's privacy?" Tessa inquired as he flipped things open and closed them again. "Isn't there some kind of law?"

"She's under twenty-one, and we have her father's permission." Griffin's tone was absent. "You know what? I'm not finding a single thing related to Trey or even a note from her girlfriends about him."

"Try the search function. It's faster." She picked up her original train of thought. "It's like reading someone's diary. An ethical thing, you know?"

He started the search function and sat back and looked at her. "An ethical thing. How ethical is it for her to let her folks think she was kidnapped? Or to run off with an older guy?"

"Two wrongs don't make a right."

"Are you preaching at me?"

Me, Ms. Woo-Woo Weirdness? Preach at you, Mr. Totally Straight and No Imagination? Yeah, right. "No. I'm just pointing it out."

He turned back to the computer when it beeped to say it had finished the task. "The whole thing is moot, anyway. There's nothing containing the word *Trey* in her mailbox. Not a very sentimental girl, our Christina."

"Most girls would keep e-mails from their guy," Tessa agreed. "The modern equivalent of tying them up in ribbon."

"Maybe she printed them out and hid them somewhere. She must not have trusted anyone."

"Turns out she was right." Tessa smiled at him. "The question is, why keep it such a deep, dark secret from her family? After all, hooking up with an executive type could be a good thing. Not my cup of tea, certainly, but it's not like he's a homeless crack dealer."

"Think about it from her point of view." Griffin closed out the screens and got up. "She's the daughter of one of the ten richest men in America. She's been living in a fishbowl her whole life. Everything she does is known, maybe not on a celebrity scale, but in Boston I know she had a companion for when she went out in public. Kind of a combination bodyguard and nanny. I think she went away when Christina turned eighteen, but you get my point."

"Maybe it's not a deep, dark secret in that way, then," Tessa mused. "Maybe she just wanted one thing that was hers, with nobody else's nose poking into it."

"So yeah, we can empathize with her, but we still have to find her. I was only half kidding about Las Vegas earlier."

"I didn't think you were kidding at all."

"So, what was that you said about the beach?"

"I want to go down there. I just have a feeling."

How far we've come, Tessa thought as he nodded and handed her a sweater. *This time yesterday if I'd said that, he would have made some nasty comment and held things up while I stumbled through yet another useless explanation. Now he just gets on with it.*

How nice it would be if he could have a little talk with Linn, and convince her that she really did have a gift.

"I want to do one thing first," she said.

"What's that?"

"I want to check the cards and see what they have to tell me. It might help me focus."

"The cards?" He looked completely at sea.

"Yes. Tarot." The velvet bag with the cards was still in her suitcase. She pulled it out of the side pocket.

"What?"

She sat on the carpet and closed her eyes. "You'll see.

Give me a moment of silence, will you?" She had the feeling he had just been temporarily rendered speechless, poor guy, so silence was not a problem.

Calming her mind, she pictured the beach and Christina, and with eyes still closed, shuffled the deck. She cut it, turned over the top card and opened her eyes.

The Ace of Cups. "Hmm."

"Hmm? Hmm what? What does it mean?"

"Would you relax? I'm not summoning a demon, Griffin. The cards are just a tool."

To her relief, he did relax. A little. "Sorry. I had a pretty conservative upbringing."

"Yeah, I got that. Well, I didn't. My mom's a painter. She did this series of nudes based on the Major Arcana—those are cards representing the stages of human experience—and her pieces are in collections all over the world. Of course, people didn't start buying them until somebody set the studio on fire. The media coverage was great."

"Was anyone hurt?"

"Oh, no. She was moving into a bigger space anyway. But it was a PR bonanza. Every single piece sold. Anyway." She returned her attention to the card. "The Ace of Cups. This card is about emotional force. Love, specifically, and more specifically still, intimacy."

"That ties in." He sounded a little hesitant, as if she'd rap him over the knuckles with a pointer if he got the wrong answer.

On the contrary. He got a gold star for playing along.

"It sure does. This card is about going with your gut, falling in love, and acting on it." She held the card up and he took it, frowning at it the way people frown at a menu in a foreign language. "See how the water is flowing out of the cup and into the lake? And the water lilies blooming on the lake? That can mean love flowing out of some-one to make something beautiful."

"O-o-kay," he said. "So that's the connection to the beach? Water?"

"Well, it helps." She took the card and returned the deck to its bag. The Queen of Wands on the exterior of the bag smiled serenely at her, and she smiled back. "But I'm betting it means something a lot more personal."

"Like what?"

"You never know for sure until you ask the person, but chances are good that Christina and Trey first made love on that beach. And that's why I've got to go there."

AS ROMANTIC PLACES WENT, the beach didn't rate very high-ly in Griffin's estimation. The northern California coastline wasn't sheltered, and the surf came rolling in sometimes seven or eight feet high, crashing on the shore with a sound and vibration like the detonation of a bomb. Little kids looked for seashells in vain; any such treasures got beaten to bits by the water long before they reached the shore.

The sustained noise of the wind and breakers had one odd effect, though. It was like that old Elton John song that talked about "solid walls of sound." The noise created an insulating effect for conversation, which couldn't be heard at all past about two feet. People could be seen, unless they were seated behind a rock or log, but they'd never be heard.

Tessa wrapped her blue sweater around her against the wind, and he briefly entertained the thought of putting an arm around her shoulder and sheltering her with his body.

He entertained the thought, and then sent it on its way. If she were going to go into another trance down here, the last thing he needed to think about was putting an arm any-where near her. In fact, he'd just keep his damn distance.

He'd stay close enough to do his duty and listen, but far enough away so that if she reached for him in the throes of a dream, he could step away to safety.

Though the sun was warm, the breeze off the combers was cool and carried the damp mist of spindrift. Tessa didn't walk where the waves creamed up on shore, but followed the line of kelp and bladder wrack at the high-tide mark, where the sand was firm but dry.

"Anything?" he asked her.

She shook her head. "I'm heading for those rocks down there."

About a quarter of a mile away, a massive chunk of granite was all that was left where the cliff had washed away and receded. Fortunately no one had built on that point of land. Griffin figured anyone who built on these cliffs had a death wish, anyway. You just couldn't guarantee that one good storm wouldn't take out your living room and deposit it in the bay.

"It's been a while since I was down here," he said.

She had a long stride, he noticed, and had no trouble keeping up with him.

With legs like that, of course she'd have a long stride.

Do not think about her legs.

Uh-huh. Or about what that gauzy purple dress does, flapping around her thighs in the breeze. You're not thinking about that, either, I bet.

No. He was doing his job.

"If I lived here, I'd be out on the beach every day," she said dreamily. "You can see the water from my apartment." She held her thumb and forefinger an inch apart. "This much of it."

"Jay used to run every morning, but the job sucks up more and more of his time."

"He should run. He needs to do something with all that stress."

"So you're in San Francisco? Your sister is, too, right? Didn't I hear she moved up there when she joined CLEU?"

Tessa nodded. "She's getting married in a few weeks. Poor thing."

"What's wrong with that? Don't like her guy?" He hadn't known Linn Nichols all that well, but he wouldn't have pegged her for the marrying kind. She was by-the-book, idealistic, and thorough to a fault. Which translated into long hours and carefully prepared cases, and that didn't mix with a developing relationship, as he knew only too well. Her guy had to be law enforcement. They tended to understand the concept of double shifts better.

"Oh, I like him, when he's not on duty and being a scary whack job. They're in narcotics," she added by way of explanation.

Griffin nodded. It explained a lot.

"No, I meant Linn has joined the demented ranks of brides-to-be. I had no idea. I never expected she would get sucked into all the magazine expectations and stuff." She shaded her eyes against the sun and gazed out to where a couple of neoprene-clad surfers were riding a big one. "If I ever take the plunge it's going to be in front of my family only, with flowers I pick on the way down to the beach."

"Better bring a microphone, then," he suggested. "You can't hear out here."

"We're a close family." She smiled at him, her dimple flashed, and he lost his train of thought. "Mostly. We'll cuddle up."

If his thoughts were ever to go in that direction, which they wouldn't, he'd probably choose the same thing.

"When I got married, I hardly saw Sheryl," he said.

"She was always surrounded by caterers and florists and bridesmaids. Both mothers. It was insane. Then the whole thing culminated in a ceremony at the biggest church in town."

But Sheryl had been happy during that time. Happy and busy and full of news every night. To him, it hadn't been the most interesting news—what did he care whether the favors were china angels or bags of potpourri?—but seeing that glow in her eyes had made it worth it.

Too bad the glow had faded when the reality of broken appliances and laundry and a budget had set in. She had wanted to do over his little house and when he'd explained that even with both their salaries, there was no extra money for a remodeled kitchen and a new bathroom, the fighting had started.

"I didn't know you were married."

He blinked and focused on Tessa again. "What, didn't see it in your crystal ball?"

"Don't have one. Too expensive."

He laughed. "I'm not now."

"Married? Or expensive?"

"Both."

Some people were project-oriented. They had to be doing things or they weren't happy. The wedding plans had made Sheryl happy in the beginning. Plans to remodel would have kept her happy once the honeymoon was over, but he hadn't figured that out yet. He had thought that he was enough—that a life together was enough.

He had been wrong.

"I'm sorry. I didn't mean to bring it up if it's a sore subject," Tessa said, coming a little closer and glancing into his face.

"Oh, it's not." Well, it wasn't a lie. Sheryl wasn't a sore

subject. She was more like a gaping wound into which he periodically poured vinegar. He thought fast for a nice, vague explanation. "Our expectations were too high. And we grew up at different rates, but we got to the same place and decided it had been a mistake."

Nice and vague, with the added advantage that it didn't resemble the truth in the least.

"How long ago did you split up?"

"What year is this?" He did some subtraction. "Six years ago." And a few months and a couple of days.

"You're just coming out of the pain zone," she said, as if she were some kind of counselor. "It takes five years to get over the chemical addiction to the other person."

"Chemical addiction? Have you been hanging around with those narcs, or what?"

"Seriously. Love produces chemicals in the brain, and you get addicted. It was in one of my psych textbooks."

"Kinda takes the romance out of it," he observed, as they arrived at the rocks. "Like this beach. Not what I would pick for a midnight tryst, what with the wind and sand and all. Getting anything yet?"

14

DRIFTWOOD HAD PILED UP around the ten-foot chunk of granite like abandoned Tinkertoys, providing shelter from the wind and the intrusive eyes of other people.

"Is that a roundabout way of saying, 'Tessa, get on with your job and stop yakking'?" she wanted to know.

"No. I don't mind your yakking." Obviously not, since he'd actually come out and spoken of something as personal as his ill-fated wedding.

"Thank you so much." She climbed over a stack of crisscrossed logs and jumped down on the other side. "Aha," she called up to him as he clambered over after her. "Here we are."

He landed in the dry sand beside her. "Here?"

It looked as if no one had been there in months, but he supposed the tide cleaned things up every night. A stretch of sand was sheltered from the wind by the rocky outcrop and the tumbled logs, and a particularly big chunk of log provided a backrest for a view out to sea.

"This is the place. Far enough from the house that she couldn't be found, and close enough to run back to before someone found out she was gone." Tessa shrugged out of her sweater and tied it around her waist. Then she sat on the sand with her back to the log and arranged her skirt over her thighs.

"So now what?" He stretched out beside her a safe couple of feet away.

"Now we open ourselves up to whatever's here." She closed her eyes, then opened them again and glanced at him. "If a crab comes up, you'll tell me, won't you?"

He tried to keep a straight face, since it was obvious she was serious. "You talk to the universe. I'll keep watch for crabs."

She settled back against the log and closed her eyes, upon which he promptly broke his promise and allowed himself to watch her instead. Sandy lashes lay on cheeks as smooth as ripe apricots, and as her mouth relaxed he saw that there was a dent in the middle of her bottom lip that invited a kiss.

This is not smart. Quit ogling her when she's not looking. You're supposed to be on crab watch.

No crab in its right mind would come and nip a human's toes. They'd only do that in self-defense. Her fear was completely irrational. And he wasn't doing any harm.

Not to her, maybe. You've got no intention of pursuing anything with her, so why are you doing this?

There was no answer to that one.

"There's a light," Tessa said dreamily.

Griffin snapped out of his self-imposed lecture and glanced at her. "A light?"

"Mmm-hmm. Coming down the beach. A flashlight. I bet it's him."

Bingo. The universe was evidently feeling chatty. This time he'd make sure there was no danger of anybody's hands being made to fondle anybody's body. He would stay objective if it killed him.

"What do you see?"

"He's staying somewhere along here." She waved a lazy hand south, farther along the beach. "Maybe with a friend."

"I thought he was local." They'd have to check that. He'd just assumed Trey lived around here, and was counting on Mandy to get a number he could match to an address to see if Christina was there. However, the way people commuted coast to coast these days, it evidently wasn't a safe assumption.

"She's been waiting for ages. On a blanket." She patted the sand. "He puts his coat around her to warm her up."

What a prince.

"She's laughing. They lie down."

"Can you hear them?"

Tessa shook her head. "Silent movies," she said, and giggled. "Or a slide show. One picture after another." She was looking at the granite outcrop as if it had a screen chipped into one side.

"He's kissing her. He's good at it, too."

"How do you know that?" Griffin blurted.

"It's what she's thinking. There's just happiness and desire everywhere. She hasn't seen him for a week or so."

Griffin decided to just shut up and hope that Tessa would tell him what was happening without being prompted.

"She wants to make love but he shakes his head. Maybe he's afraid someone will surprise them. Now he's touching her. Just a little. Then he'll go."

Griffin had touched Tessa just a little, too, and look what had happened there. The memory seemed to be embedded in his fingertips and the palms of his hands, no matter how hard he tried to make it go away.

"She wore the silk teddy he gave her last time. He pulls it up and leans down and licks her nipple."

Oh, God. Could a person pull the plug on the movie? Did he need to hear this?

"She loves to drive him crazy with the things she wears. Next time they go out it will be the taupe dress. She wants to trap him in the elevator at Atlantis and make love in public."

Griffin gulped. Because it wasn't Christina he was seeing. It wasn't some disembodied vision made of flashes in the dark. It was himself he was seeing, doing things like that with Tessa.

Tessa, who at this moment was wearing a gauzy little Indian-cotton dress like the ones the hippie chicks in Santa Rita wore. Beads sparkled along the deeply cut *U* of the neckline and as she leaned forward, watching her internal movie, her curves pressed insistently against the fabric.

Then he blinked. It wasn't just curves. Her nipples were rigid, poking at the fragile cotton in a way that begged for the satisfaction of a man's hands.

Of a man's mouth. His mouth.

His body tingled all over as hot blood rushed to his groin. His cock stiffened and he lost the ability to think about anything but the way the sparkly fabric of her dress held back those smooth, creamy curves.

"Griffin?" She rolled on one hip to face him, her bare knee pressing against his denim-clad thigh. "Are you okay?"

"Huh?" He dragged his gaze from her cleavage to her face. "Is it over?"

"They started to make love and the picture sort of fuzzed out. That happens, you know. When you make love. You lose touch with the external world."

"Do you?" He couldn't remember, it had been so long.

"You get so wrapped up in the other person…in their mouth…in their hands…you know?"

She was sun-warmed and sensual and every word was like another match to a piece of paper already on fire. Her mouth was so close and it was saying those things and he just…couldn't…help it….

TESSA'S LIPS PARTED under his like a tropical flower opening to the sun. The heat of his desire washed over her and she responded to it as naturally as if her body had been waiting for his all along.

All the good sense in the world told her this man was wrong for her. They came from different backgrounds, had different definitions of just about every principle and had different expectations of life.

Yup, she should listen to good sense.

But not while his mouth tasted so good. Not while his heat burned her, while his hands slid around her and dragged her closer. His tongue invaded her mouth and slid along hers, inviting and asking permission at the same time. She stroked it in response and he deepened the kiss, changing his angle so that it tipped her head back.

A tiny sound slipped from her throat, a sound that was two parts desire and one part surrender. Griffin broke the kiss and looked into her eyes.

"I did it again." He straightened, and the cool air flowed between them, chilling the parts that had been fused together.

"Did what again?" She couldn't seem to take her gaze off his mouth. He had a great mouth, and he knew exactly what to do with it. She loved that in a man.

"It's this case." His gesture seemed to encompass both her and the trysting spot. "Every time you see them, they're making love. I'm supposed to be helping you see details about where they are, and instead I let the sex distract me."

"I like distracting you." She moved closer, and put a hand on his chest. The fabric of his shirt was heated from the sun and from his agitation.

It was exciting to be the reason for that agitation. She just had to find a way to get him past this idea that sex was a problem and move on to the good part. After all, they were alone in this sheltered spot and both of them wanted the same thing.

She took his chin in her fingers, turned his head and captured his lips with hers.

His resistance crumbled like a sand castle against the tide. *Yes, I'm giving you permission,* her mouth said, *so stop teasing and get down to business.*

He might not be a sensitive, but he knew a thing or two about body language. This time his kiss was deep and less restrained, as if he'd allowed himself to enjoy it. Her arms slid around his neck and she slid across him to straddle his lap as he sat with his back against the log.

"Now, then," she said happily, and he raised his mouth to meet hers once more. *Is that permission enough for you?* He drank kisses from her, and now his was the head tipped back against the scarred, weathered wood. Maybe he got tired of being in charge all the time. Maybe he just needed a girl to tell him to shut up and kiss her.

For the moment, Tessa was perfectly happy to be that girl.

His hands were heavy at her waist, as if he felt he had to hold her down, and their heat burned through the fabric of her dress. That wasn't all that was burning. Pressing against her damp panties was the evidence that this was no ordinary kiss. His erection was hard and insistent, and every time she moved, his hips lifted in glorious suggestion.

The atmosphere of this spot was finally getting to him.

Her thighs hugged his hips and her crotch fit onto his erection through two layers of underwear and one of denim. She rocked against it, slowly, the rhythm as ancient as the crash of the waves or the pull of the tide.

"We shouldn't be doing this," he groaned. "Christina is depending on us."

Tessa stroked the long line of his lower lip with her tongue and bit it gently. "I don't think she's thinking about us at all," she said against his lips. "I want you to undo my zipper."

"Oh, God." His head fell back against the log in a posture of temporary defeat, but she felt his erection throb and tighten.

"I know you want to look at my breasts," she whispered wickedly. "And the sun is so hot—you're so hot—I want your mouth on me, Griffin."

He made a sound in the back of his throat and lowered his mouth to her cleavage as he skimmed his hands up her rib cage and cupped her breasts in both hands. His mouth was hot and demanding and bolts of pleasure flickered through her as he licked her skin.

Since her hands were free, Tessa reached around and ran her zipper down its track herself. The fragile fabric relaxed, and the neckline dropped, exposing her nipples.

"Damn," he whispered. "No bra. You *do* read minds. Or answer prayers."

With a shimmy of her shoulders, the dress dropped completely to her waist, where her sweater was tied, leaving her naked to his gaze. And what a gaze it was. It devoured her, worshipped her, consumed her like fire and left her hotter than ever.

"You prayed I wouldn't wear a bra?" She smiled with delight and anticipation.

"Yeah, well, call me shallow. You are the most beautiful thing I ever laid eyes on."

"Lick me," she commanded softly. "I want your mouth on my nipples."

"Another prayer answered."

Her nipples felt rigid with impatience, as though she couldn't wait for his mouth to lower that last inch and taste her. When he did, when the damp heat of his tongue swirled around her areola and his lips closed on her, she moaned. She wasn't the only one who was impatient. He suckled her hard, tugging gently, both hands holding her breasts with a kind of reverence. The pleasure spread like wildfire through her body, a bolt of lightning that ignited the very core of her and made it weep with need for him.

As if he were the one who read minds, he slid one hand under the skirt of her dress and stroked her naked thighs. "Your skin is like silk," he murmured into her cleavage as his tongue made a slow trip down one slope and up the other. With stealth, he stroked her inner thighs with those long fingers that seemed to be designed for this very thing.

"Will you touch me?" she whispered. "I'm so wet for you I can't stand it."

His mouth closed on her other nipple, drawing it deeply into his mouth where his tongue flickered over it and made her whimper.

"Please, Griffin."

In answer, his fingers stroked the damp crotch of her panties. She was so swollen and sensitive that she jumped at the eruption of pleasure from his touch.

"Please," she begged breathlessly. Oh, would he stop teasing? How could she get his jeans off without breaking the moment? How long could she stand not having him inside her?

"Who's in charge now?" he murmured against her skin, his cheek creasing in a wicked grin. Meanwhile, his fingers teased her, featherlight, dancing along her vulva through the aggravating protection of her panties.

"You are," she panted. "Don't stop."

He had mercy on her then, and slid his hand under the low-slung waistband of her panties, cupping her mound and sliding a finger into her folds. She moaned with pleasure.

"I am, huh? Okay, how about this?"

Before she realized what he was doing, he'd stripped off his T-shirt and tossed it on the log behind his head. Then, with an arm under her knees and one under her shoulders, he lifted her bodily onto the fabric-covered log.

Oh, my. "Are you going to—here—what if—?"

He covered her mouth in a kiss that obliterated all ability to ask questions. Then he kissed his way down her supine body and with one movement, pulled off her panties. She found a foothold for one foot on another, lower log and gasped as he moved between her legs.

She forgot the sea breeze that cooled her moist pussy, as wet as a bed of damp moss. She forgot the blazing sun and the possibility of discovery. She even forgot her no-cops rule and the knowledge that she shouldn't be doing this with a man who was so wrong for her.

But who cared, when his mouth was hot and masterful on her thighs, when his tongue was skilled, when reality was even better than her late-night fantasies?

He separated her folds with those wicked fingers and lowered his mouth to her clitoris. With the first stroke of his tongue she practically came up off the log. He held her down and imprisoned her with his mouth, giving pleasure and demanding response with every fierce stroke. She was so ready, so suffused with need, that three or four strokes were all it took.

She cried out, high and ecstatic, as the orgasm crashed through her, radiating out from his tongue through every muscle and fiber.

He cried out, too, and tore his mouth away from her shuddering body. He pulled her skirts down with such abruptness that she swung herself to a sitting position and practically fell into his arms.

"Oh, my God, Griffin, that was—"

"Pull your dress up."

"What?" Dazed with pleasure, glowing with satisfaction, her muscles were so relaxed she could hardly sit up straight.

"Quick! There's a dog."

She gawked at the huge black Labrador who was panting next to him. He'd obviously just goosed Griffin in a sensitive spot and he stood there, ready to play, wearing a grin as big and goofy as her own had just been.

"Oh, no."

The zipper screeched up its track just in time. Two preteen boys burst around the foot of the granite outcrop, calling for the dog, and coming up short when they saw the two of them.

Tessa and Griffin sat side by side on the log, as innocent as two strangers on a park bench.

The boys goggled at them, called the dog's name, then turned and ran back the way they had come, the dog bounding after them.

Too late, Tessa saw her underwear lying on the sand.

Oops.

Maybe they'd think it was a jellyfish.

15

NORMALLY YOU COULD EXPECT a guy who had just given you fabulous oral sex to take your hand on the way back down the beach.

But no-o-o-o-o.

Clearly, Griffin had been jolted off that happy track and back into his serious, on-the-job rut. "Tessa, we need to talk."

"Okay." She smiled at him, but he wouldn't meet her eyes.

"Jay is depending on us. So until we find Christina, we can't let ourselves get sidetracked by—" He stopped.

"Ourselves?"

"By anything. Including this—" he moved his hands, as if trying to describe it "—this thing that keeps happening between us."

"I don't know about you, but I like this thing," she said cheerfully. "It's a man and a woman enjoying what comes naturally. What's wrong with that?"

"Nothing, except that we're not the right man or the right woman."

Oh, well, if you put it *that* way.

She knew it. Really, she did. But it was depressing to have it pointed out so...pointedly. Obviously, there was something about sex or women or sex with this woman in particular that frightened Mr. Former Hardnosed Cop to death.

What a shame. All that great potential, going to waste. Despite what he said, she just couldn't let it happen. Maybe she should push him a bit more. Like a counselor would. Take him past the point of no return so he could see it wasn't as scary as he thought on the other side.

Not that she was thinking along the lines of anything permanent, mind you. But since they were here and stuck with each other and thinking about sex as much as they thought about the case, what could be wrong with going with the flow?

Maybe she should throw the cards.

Maybe she should talk to her sister. See what she knew about Griffin Knox and his ex-wife.

Maybe you should mind your own business.

Hey, he'd just made her come. That made it her business.

And what happens if the flow turns into a raging river and you can't get out?

Ha! She should be so lucky.

Be careful what you wish for.

LINN WAS OUT on surveillance, one of her sister's coworkers told her once she was back in Christina's room. Griffin was with Jay, hopefully *not* briefing him on their personal take on the beach scene in *From Here to Eternity,* so she had a few minutes to get the scoop on him.

"Can you do me a favor and look up the number for Natalie Wong at the Santa Rita P.D.?"

"Sure. Is this Linn's sister?"

"Yes. And who is this?"

"Coop. Cooper Maxwell," he elaborated when she didn't respond.

"Oh, Coop. Hi." *Eek*. Maybe she should just call SRPD directly.

"I hear we're going to be walking down the aisle together."

She distinctly felt her heart stop, trip, and then start up again. "What?"

"You and me. Maid of honor and best man. You know, during the ceremony."

"Oh. Oh, yeah. I knew that. Can't wait," she lied.

"That is, if we all make it in one piece to the ceremony. I don't know if I can stand another month of this."

"Is Linn getting on everyone's nerves? Holding swatches of lavender silk up against you and stuff?"

"No, she's just really, really stressed. That woman took down a drug lord with a bottle of wine, but one call from the caterer can reduce her to tears."

"Wow. That's bad. Um, I'm a little short on time, here. Can I get that number?"

"Oh, sure. Hey, I'll tell her you called. God knows she needs someone female to talk to. Okay, this card here says Natalie Wong is in Forensics. Direct line is 831-555-7725."

"Thanks, Investigator."

"Girls I walk down aisles with call me Coop."

"Coop. Right. Bye."

Tessa disconnected, feeling as though she'd escaped some kind of trap. Okay, Natalie Wong. She dialed the number, and to her relief, Natalie picked up right away and even remembered her.

"Oh, sure, Linn's sister. We met at my Dirty Thirties birthday bash."

"That's right. It was fun. Hey, um, I need some personal information and since Linn is on surveillance I thought I would go right to the source."

"As long as it's not case-related, I'm your girl."

"Oh, it's not. Not your case, anyway. Did you know a guy called Griffin Knox?"

"Sure I knew him. Got his knee blown out by a crack-head. Invalided out. Works for some corporation now, but I can't remember which one."

"Ocean Technology."

"Yes, that was it. What did you need to know?"

"How well did you know him? And are you still in touch?"

"As well as I know any of these guys, and no. He kind of fell off the face of the earth as far as the department was concerned. Doesn't even come to the Christmas party, though I know for a fact the chief's assistant invites him every year."

Oh, good. That meant Natalie wasn't likely to ring him up and have a chummy chat about how Tessa was checking up on him.

"Do you know anything about his, um, personal life?"

There was a pause, and Tessa imagined Natalie tilting her head and narrowing her eyes. "Any particular reason you need to know?"

She was not a good liar, and there wasn't much point in learning to be a better one now. "I'm in a—a situation with him. An attraction thing. But he keeps pulling back and I need to know if there's a reason for it. I figure the ex-wife is probably a good place to start."

"You mean Sheryl."

"Um, yeah."

A few beats of silence passed during which Natalie appeared to be thinking. Or maybe she'd just decided that Tessa was way too nosy about a former fellow officer and she was deciding on a nice way to tell her to get lost. Or maybe—

"See, the thing with Griffin is that he was head over heels about his wife," Natalie said slowly. "I can trust you not to pass this on, right?"

"Absolutely," Tessa promised.

"That's the kind of guy he is. Intense. Persistent. When he goes for something, he does it one hundred percent, whether it's an investigation or a relationship or whatever. So when he married Sheryl, as far as he was concerned, he was in it for life. You should have heard the way he talked about her."

"How long were they married?"

"Three years."

"Not very long."

"Like I say, he was in it for life. It's a shame she didn't see things the same way."

Aha. Now they were coming to it. "What happened?"

Natalie paused. "I feel like such a gossip. Are you sure you shouldn't be talking this over with Griffin?"

"We're not at the point where you go through the ex list." *We're not at any point at all, really, beach orgasm notwithstanding.* "But this is really helping."

"You're probably wondering how I know all this."

"Yeah, kind of. He doesn't strike me as the type to bare his heart to his coworkers."

"He wasn't, but Sheryl was."

"Ah. Linn said you worked with her."

"She was our admin, so we analysts got the instant replay every morning during their courtship, the engagement, the wedding plans, you name it. I even helped her pick her colors. And then when Griffin got shot, we were as supportive as we could be. Until it started going a little weird."

"Weird?"

"Yeah." Natalie sighed. "You know, in-house romances are really a bad idea, especially in police departments. And when you have a talker like Sheryl, there are no secrets."

"I can imagine."

"Sheryl and Griffin's partner spent a lot of time in the hospital with him. And then they started spending a lot of time out of it."

Tessa saw where this was going. "Uh-oh."

"Yup. She left him for his partner. Caleb resigned and took a job with Sacramento P.D., and that's where they're living now. I have no idea how much contact there is between Griffin and Sheryl, but when it all went down, he was completely shattered."

"No kidding. And all this happened six years ago?"

"More or less."

"Wow. Well, thanks, Natalie. This helps me understand him better."

"I hope so. Because I wouldn't get my hopes up too high, you know."

"What do you mean?"

"Oh, he didn't swear off women or anything. That would be a simple way to deal with it. From what I've heard from a couple of the girls who tried to comfort him in his loss, he's just not emotionally available."

"Still hung up on Sheryl?"

"It's hard to say. But between us girls, just watch your heart."

Yeah, she'd figured that one out on her own.

Tessa thanked Natalie, hung up and reached for her tarot deck. With Griffin and his story filling her mind, she asked the universe for some guidance, cut the deck and chose a card.

The King of Swords.

Why was she not surprised?

This card was about a man of intellect who worked with information using the active, outward focus of the leader. She couldn't have picked a card that described Griffin better. Truthful, impartial, analytical—and a man who acted on what he believed. So, actions were called for here. But what kind? Thinking up a solution? Yep, definitely. Communicating? He was in the house doing that right now. But what about with her? The only thing he communicated was desire, and his intellect was busy shutting that down.

Hmm. Tessa shuffled again, cut, and pulled another card.

The Hierophant. Okay, that symbolized institutions and their values. Like police departments. And marriage. Members of institutions are rewarded for following convention, though in the case of the latter that hadn't really worked out for Griffin. But what did the card mean for her? Simply that she was up against a force that was not innovative, free-spirited or individual like herself? Or that she needed to get with the program, whatever that was?

She shuffled again and pulled a third card. The Ten of Pentacles.

Tessa sat back with a sense of accomplishment. Well, as her mom used to say, that tied it. The Ten of Pentacles was a reinforcing card to the Hierophant. It meant material success, as evidenced by all the coins floating in the air in the marketplace scene on the card, but it also meant seeking permanence and following convention.

In Griffin's case, though, it might mean something deeper. Natalie Wong had said he wasn't emotionally available. But maybe he was looking for a longer-term solution than what the girls at the office had offered. The card confirmed that he still wanted to create a lasting foundation in his relationships, that he craved being "in it for life."

There was hope for the guy yet. But did that mean she was part of the solution?

Tessa gathered up the cards and slid them into their bag. Permanence and convention had never been part of her life plan. Whatever the universe had in mind for Griffin Knox, her part was to help him solve this case—and, she thought wickedly, maybe loosen up that oh-so-stiff spine of his.

Maybe she'd pave the way for some dignified long-term woman to walk in and make the guy happy.

It certainly wasn't going to be her.

16

From the private journal of Jay Singleton

I can't believe it. Trey Ludovic. A guy I like(d), a guy who's been in my own home, drunk my scotch, sat at my table.

That *bastard*.

It all falls into place now. I flew Christina out here on the company jet for Christmas, had that costume made for her…and then she meets him at the Christmas party. She calls me in February and asks me to send her an application for UC Santa Rita. Like a big dumb trout, I snap up the bait and say that if she's interested, she can just move out here. She's here by April, all expenses paid, and voilà, they're together, courtesy of dear old Dad.

Griffin says there's no evidence in her laptop that indicates they had an online affair, but that doesn't mean anything. They could have built a private chat room and met there a dozen times a day.

I swear, I'm going to kill him. But first, I'm going to talk to Mandy. I'm spoiling for a fight, and by God, this is it. If he's going to take my daughter, I'm going to take his company. I'm gonna redefine the "hostile" in "hostile take-over." Mandy will know exactly how to position it with the SEC and with Stellar Memory's board.

Trey Ludovic is going to be massively sorry he ever set eyes on my daughter.

NOW WOULD BE a good time for a software pirate to hack into Ocean Technology's server farm.

Griffin cruised past the condo complex half a mile down the beach from the Singleton property, where supposedly Stellar Memory had a company suite. After showing his ID at the gatehouse, he parked the truck in a guest space and gazed at the tumble of Spanish-style cubes zigzagging down the hillside. In the quiet of the night, tastefully illuminated by lamps hidden in the shrubbery, you'd never guess the units went for a million or more each.

Yeah, a pirate would be great. A spectacular crime like a hack job would give him a perfect excuse to get the hell out of here and back to some semblance of a normal life.

A life that didn't contain a blond psychic with a kissable mouth and a body to die for. Who wore gauzy dresses and short skirts and had no idea of the havoc she created inside him simply by walking up a flight of stairs.

It was a case of deprivation, that was all. It had been months since he'd had the time or inclination to pursue anyone. His last affair, with one of the software engineers who had been a witness in the breach of a nondisclosure agreement, had lasted six months and then fizzled from lack of interest.

Griffin sighed and got out of the truck, landing with most of his weight on his right leg to spare his aching left knee. The important thing here was not his body and what happened to it when Tessa got anywhere near him. In the cold light of reality, he'd meant what he'd said to Tessa this afternoon. The important thing was finding Christina.

The super of the building was unusually helpful, probably due to Griffin's Ocean Tech ID and the fact that everyone in Carmel knew Jay Singleton. In twenty minutes he was back at the truck, in possession of three facts: one, that Trey Ludovic was indeed using the company condo; two, he'd recently purchased a house in Carmel Valley; and three, that he was out of town—where, the super didn't know.

Griffin had hoped the super would let him into the suite, but without a police badge and a warrant, the guy had every right to give him that "Are you kidding? I'd lose my job for that" look and say no.

Griffin fired up the truck and headed back up the highway. So Tessa's vision checked out—again. It had been perfectly possible for Ludovic to stroll down the beach and meet Christina at the rocky outcrop. But fact-checking wasn't getting them any closer to finding the girl. He had to figure out some way of getting Tessa to focus on details—and not of the two runaways making love, either. He needed details of their surroundings that would lead him to a real place, somewhere they could go to convince Christina to come home.

If she wanted to.

Griffin shook off that thought. One thing at a time. And the first thing was Tessa.

Back at the estate a few minutes later, he found her in the cottage in front of the laptop. She had evidently taken advantage of his absence to shower and change into the cotton bottoms and tank top she slept in.

He willed himself to focus on the back of her head, where her hair was drying into a wavy bob. "Working on the case?"

Tessa sat back. "No, just checking my e-mail. I wanted to send a thank-you note to Na—to someone. For something they did for me. Um, how'd it go? Did you find where he lives?"

"Yep." Griffin sat on the end of the bed and kept his gaze resolutely on her hair. No lower. "Stellar Memory has a company condo about half a mile south—via the highway. It's closer if you use the beach. He's not there."

"That would be way too easy."

"I didn't think we'd find them holed up there, but it had to be checked out. The super says Ludovic bought a house, though, so he won't be in the condo much longer."

"A house." She hugged one knee and rocked back in the chair. "I did some more surfing around. He's from Houston originally, so the condo was probably temporary housing when he took on the job here. Looks like he's going to make it permanent."

"That'll make Jay happy. No chance of bribing the guy to go back to Houston and pick on someone his own age if he's laid out a couple of mil for a place here."

A silence fell. Tessa shifted uncomfortably on the chair, and then got up and pulled on her blue sweater, hiding the tank top but not the spectacular curves under it. She was dressed exactly the same way she had been the first time he'd—

Stop, he commanded his memory. Don't even go there.

Tessa took a step toward him, then two more. "She wants to know if he's coming," she said.

He stared at her. "Coming where?"

"To bed, silly." She smoothed her hands down the curves of breast and hip. "She got some new lingerie today."

She's looking at Christina. His skin prickled. *Shazam. Just like that.*

Griffin got to his feet carefully, so as not to startle Tessa out of Christina's reality. "Come on over here," he said softly.

She let him lead her to the bed, where he sat beside her. "What does the room look like?"

Her gaze tracked from left to right. "They're sitting on a big couch in front of a window. There's a chair that matches it over there." She gestured to the left, where the laptop sat on its table. "It's covered in something striped. Blue and white. There's a table between, with nothing on it. Um, what else?" She wrinkled her forehead. "A bookcase. A kitchen door, that way." She waved her other hand to the right. "Um, a rug."

"You're doing great. Can you see a motel sign through the window?"

"A motel sign? Outside the house? No."

"You're in a house, not a motel? Where?"

Tessa giggled. "She wants to make out, right there on the couch. She wants him to pretend he's eighteen, too. Like this."

And before he could think of a way to distract her or bring her out of the trance, Tessa had wrapped her arms around his neck and pressed her lips to his.

This is too weird. Stop. Stop it. He wrenched his mouth away. "Tessa. Wait."

"She's not into delayed gratification." She caught him off balance and pushed him backward onto the bed, where she climbed on top of him, her body measuring the length of his.

His erection was not as fussy as his brain about whose reality this woman was in. It reacted enthusiastically to the pressure of her pubis and he groaned. "Wait—"

"She says, 'Look at this, beautiful man. Check out what two hundred bucks will get you.'"

Still lying on top of him, she whipped the blue sweater off over her head and flopped down on him again. Slowly, she writhed so that the weight of her breasts, naked under the tank top but presumably, in her mind, in some kind of fancy bra, teased him. "She says, 'How do you like it?'"

He had no answer. Because in that moment, sprawled on him in sexy abandon, Tessa Nichols came back.

WARM. HARD. She was lying full length on a man's body.

Griffin's body.

Griffin's *aroused* body.

Tessa came out of the vision the way a diver rises to the surface of the ocean, through graduating layers of clarity. She was stretched out on top of him, her breasts flattened against his chest and her legs on either side of his. His lips were parted in a combination of pleasure and distress, mirroring the chaotic state of his emotions.

The distress was mostly in his head, a pale curtain of agitation that gained color and heat as it got closer to the source of his pleasure buried under her hips. This was intellect at war with inclination again, and she'd be willing to bet on which one was going to win. Especially if—since she was in this position anyway—she helped it along a little.

"Tessa—" he rasped.

"Shut up and kiss me," she said with soft command. Short of being thrown off him with sheer brute strength, she was more than a match for his stuffy old intellect. Especially when it was perfectly obvious that his pleasure was working on her side.

With her elbows bracketing his head, she moved in and kissed him. His lips remained stiff for about half a second as he debated on what he was going to do, and then it seemed as though he decided to just go with the moment. Or maybe his body's demand was shouting louder than his brain's need for caution.

Whatever. She didn't care what was going on inside that cop's mind of his. She was just going to kiss him for all she was worth.

"Mmm." A sound of pure pleasure escaped her throat as his tongue met hers and slid its length in welcome. His lips were mobile and firm, and knew exactly how to woo and tease, and finally, how to take charge.

He slid both hands around her waist, then stroked down over her derriere, learning its shape. Then he held her as he rolled to the side and slid one arm under her head as a pillow.

"I thought we decided this wasn't a good idea," he whispered.

Which would be fine if his gaze wasn't tracing the contours of her mouth as though he couldn't wait to taste it again.

"You may have decided," she said. "I like it."

"But it's not a good idea to—"

She put a finger on his lips. "Stop thinking. And parts of you think it's a great idea. Trust me. I know."

"Parts of me are highly undependable." Even as he spoke, his hand wandered from her hip to her waist to her rib cage, hovered, then moved south again as if sticking by some internal resolution.

Ha. I know what you want.

She laid her hand over his and guided it north again,

slowly. Sliding over ribs and fabric. Arriving at its destination.

"Tessa," he breathed, and closed his eyes as he cupped her breast. She released him and sighed with pleasure as the heat of his hand covered her and his thumb teased her nipple into a pebble of delight.

He lowered his head and nuzzled the curves of her cleavage above the scoop neck of the tank top. "This is wrong," he groaned, and pulled the neckline down with his thumb so he could thrust his tongue deeply into the valley between her breasts. "I shouldn't be doing this." His tongue swirled over her skin.

"No," she agreed with a sigh of pleasure. Was there anything this man's mouth couldn't do well?

He pulled up her tank top by its hem and tugged it off over her head. "Absolutely not," he breathed. "Damn, you stun me every time." He gazed at her naked breasts in the lamplight. "A visual feast."

"Eat me," she suggested breathlessly, and he lowered his head and bit her nipple gently.

She took a deep breath, forcing her nipple into his mouth, and he suckled it, each caress of his tongue sending pleasure careening through her, arrowing down to that dark, wet place between her legs.

He seemed to lose control a little, but then, so did she, as his hungry mouth devoured her, suckling fiercely, tugging at her flesh, and then assuaging any hurt by soft laps of his tongue. She could die like this, she thought, drowning in the adulation of his mouth, the pleasure of tongue and teeth and hot, hungry eyes.

"Your nipples drive me crazy," he said against her skin. "And I'm becoming obsessed with what you wear."

"Bad policeman," she chided. "What are you doing, thinking about my nipples when you're supposed to be working?"

"Can't help it," he said. "You look like every man's fantasy."

She rather doubted that, considering the state of her love life, but it was marvelously obvious that she was *his* fantasy. And that was fine. She was completely prepared to be his dream lover, even if it didn't go any further. It wasn't every day a girl was treated to a mouth like his.

Her skin craved the contact of something other than his shirt and jeans. She undid the buttons of his shirt, slowly, taking time to touch the planes of each muscle in his chest and marvel at the mat of hair she found there. When she got to the buttons at the bottom where the shirt was tucked in, she pushed him gently onto his back.

Now it was her turn to taste the shape of him, to run tongue and teeth gently over the ripples of his abs, to taste where she had touched before. She nibbled happily on his erect nipples, then coasted down again to swirl her tongue around his belly button.

He made a gasping sound that might have been her name and she smiled against his skin. Then with a twist of her fingers, she undid the button on the waistband of his jeans and slid the zipper down. Each of its teeth gave a tiny click as it opened, revealing another fraction of skin and then the band of his briefs. The heel of her hand rested on the bulge of his erection, and she could feel the tremor in his muscles as he willed himself not to move. At last the zipper reached the end of its track and she spread the placket wide, cupping her palm over his penis.

He jumped and sucked air past his teeth.

"These need to come off," she suggested.

Wordlessly, he lifted his hips and stripped off jeans and underwear, and then rolled her on top of him. "Where was that going?" he growled.

"Oh, nowhere." She batted innocent eyes. "I was just exploring."

"I bet you were. Find anything interesting?"

"Mmm. Very."

"Are you going to keep going?"

A thrill of anticipation tiptoed through her at the admission. Some part of her really thought he'd stop her, or at least find some reason to get up and leave. But he seemed to be as eager to have her as she was to have him. She could work with that.

"Absolutely," she promised.

"In that case, I have a question," he said.

Tessa made herself comfortable on his chest, and stroked his ankles with her bare toes. "Mmm?"

"Are you on birth control? Because the condoms in my truck are a year old."

"Guess it's time to replace them." She smiled into his eyes. "Go on. Be an optimist. If you buy new condoms, sex will come."

"But meantime?"

She explored the tender skin below his ear with her tongue. "Yes. I'm on birth control." To straighten out some irregular periods, but no way was she going to bring boring clinical details in at the moment. "What about you? Should I get out my predate contract with the check boxes and doctor's signature?" She nipped his earlobe.

His chest shook as he chuckled. "No need. I'm clean. And it's been so long for me I think they reissued my virgin card."

"Ooh. I've always wanted to make love with a virgin."

"Then this is your lucky day."

17

GRIFFIN ROLLED TESSA onto her back and stripped off his shirt and her pajama bottoms, then took a moment to drink her in. He wasn't going to ask about who her partners were. In the long term, it didn't matter. If she was single and on birth control, she could sleep with whomever she wanted to and it was none of his business.

His business right now was pleasure—hers and his.

He lowered his head and began to drop kisses along her collarbone, ending at that enchanting dip at the base of her throat that begged for a kiss.

This was not forever. Both of them knew it. But with any luck, making love with her would release the pressure cooker of desire that had built between them whether he wanted it to or not. Maybe, once they had possessed each other, he could get a grip again and concentrate on his job without being distracted every time she bent over or her skirt brushed his legs as she passed.

Her body called to him now, demanding that he stop thinking for once and just lose himself in it. She stroked his shoulders and arms, her touch featherlight and teasing, while he licked and nuzzled his way down her chest and over each beautiful breast. He loved the shape of her, the smooth lower curves as full as ripe fruit, the berry pucker of her nipples as they tightened under his lips. The skin was unbelievably soft on her stomach, with the strength of toned muscles underneath, and dipped inward on an indrawn breath as he reached her navel and prepared to move lower.

"No fair," she whispered. "You wouldn't let me taste you. I still owe you one."

Something had stopped him, as if her taking him in her mouth would be too intimate or leave him too helpless in her hands. He couldn't analyze his reasons right now, not with the siren call of need in his blood and the sweet taste of her on his tongue.

"All's fair," he managed, and slid around to reposition himself between her legs.

"But I—no, wait—oh!"

He parted her thighs and tongued her vulva boldly. He wouldn't have thought that his erection could get any stiffer, but the scent of the creamy liquid ready and waiting for him seemed to set off a chemical explosion inside him. At least he could guarantee she was comfortable. When he'd taken her this way on the log, it had been hard to block out the worry that she would slip off or they would be discovered or she would be too cold.

Now it was just him and her and the night.

Helpless whimpers issued from her throat as he tongued her sensitive folds, long strokes making her thighs quiver in response. At the apex he found her clitoris and settled on it, his tongue working in a rhythm that made her breathing speed up in counterpoint.

The scent of her filled his head the way the textures of her skin and the damp, secret places of her body created a kaleidoscope of pleasure for him. He loved this sense of discovery about all the places his tongue could go that pleased her.

"Oh—oh—Griffin. Don't stop—don't—yes—yes—"

She convulsed under his mouth and he gripped her thighs, milking the orgasm from her as she tried to stifle a scream in the pillow.

She was still gasping when he came up for air, his senses filled with the gift of her pleasure and the taste of completion.

"Take me now," she begged, spreading her legs wide to grip him as he stretched over her. His erection was a fiery ache, an imperative it was impossible to deny.

It was equally impossible to deny Tessa's need. She took him in both hands to guide him to her wet entrance, and wrapped her legs around his hips. She was tight, making him shiver with need as he probed her opening, a little farther each time. Then, with a long thrust he slid inside her and his mind went blank of everything except the slick pleasure of her body and the hot, demanding clasp that sheathed him.

"You feel so good," he gasped.

The grip of her thighs encouraged him to plunge deeper, to stroke harder, and her hips lifted to meet his with every move.

The pleasure built deep inside him, starting at his spine, then advancing in a heavy wave, blasting through testicles and cock and crashing into a climax so intense he thought he would black out.

Her name sounded in his head, and filled his skull, riding the wave of satisfaction.

TESSA WOKE FEELING COLD. With her eyes still shut, unwilling to come completely out of the cocoon of sleep, she slid one hand flat under the covers, fingers expecting to encounter the warmth of Griffin's body.

Nothing. This bed must be really wide.

She opened her eyes as she rolled to the side, and saw nothing but a big empty space where he should have been. She sat up and looked around the cottage's bedroom/living room combination. There was no sound but the boom of the breakers outside and the bass buzz of a pair of hummingbirds flying in circles around each other in a trumpet vine outside the window.

He'd gone home. He hadn't wanted to wake up next to her.

Well, what did you expect?

The sparkle kind of went out of the day after that. Tessa pulled on a denim mini and a pale-purple T-shirt advertising the San Francisco Blues Festival from two years ago, and shoved her feet into her flip-flops. Then she crossed the patio to the main house to see just how far Griffin Knox had run.

To her surprise, he hadn't climbed in his truck and blasted off for parts unknown. She heard voices coming from Jay's office, and pushed open the door to see the two of them hovering over the desk, looking at a piece of paper with lines drawn on it.

"Good morning." She helped herself to the carafe of coffee on the sideboard. One thing about the service here—whoever made the coffee really knew what they were doing. At least there was one thing she could count on to be where it was supposed to be in the morning.

"Tessa." Jay greeted her with a nod and a smile.

A smile?

"Hey, kiddo," Griffin said with gruff geniality.

Kiddo?

Just a few hours ago he had been making her clitoris delirious and now she was *kiddo?* What the hell was going on?

He's running in place, her instinct told her. Just like a man. He'd spent most of a week craving her, and then once he had her, he was doing everything he could to distance himself from what they'd created together. Maybe he couldn't deny what had happened, but he sure could prevent it happening again. And a really effective way to do that was to relegate her to the status of kid sister, right in front of a witness who was also employing both of them.

Oh, he was good. But then, according to Natalie, he'd had lots of practice at it.

You win this round, you big fraud. But unlike you, I know what the cards say. You want to connect with someone. You just don't want yourself to want it.

It was clear her mission was to loosen up this guy. Get him comfortable with relating to women again. Convince the King of Swords he could put down the blade that warded everybody off, and enjoy life a little.

Little did he know that the Queen of Wands was more than a match for him.

"Good morning." She mimicked his genial tone so well he probably didn't know she was being sarcastic. "What's up?"

"Griffin tells me you saw Christina again last night, and got some details of where they are," Jay said. "Good work."

"I drew a layout." Griffin pushed the piece of paper toward her. "Does this look anything like what you remember?"

The warm scent of the coffee soothed her as she joined them, sipping from the mug. On the paper he had drawn the outline of a room, with slash lines for doorways and the furniture sketched in.

His body temperature seemed to increase as she leaned over his shoulder, making her aware that he was freshly showered and deliciously clean. The scent of his subtle cologne—a scent that fell somewhere between musk and wood shavings—teased her nose.

Yum.

Nice try at going all businesslike on me. I can still make your thermometer pop.

"There was a low square table here." She pointed to the corner of the *L* made by couch and chair. With a couple of strokes, Griffin drew it in.

"And a potted plant—one of those dragon plants, you know, tall, with long pointed leaves—was here." She pointed to the slashes labeled *kitchen* and Griffin scratched in something that looked like a lion's mane that had been in the dryer too long. Okay, so he hadn't been an art major. *Plant,* he wrote beside it.

"Anything else?" Jay asked.

"What's this?"

Tessa looked up to see Mandy, dressed in a white sheath and ivory bangles, sipping her own coffee and craning over the desk.

"Tessa saw Christina and Trey again last night, and we were able to get some details," Griffin explained briefly. "They're in a house, apparently, and this is the layout of the room." He pointed. "Couch, chair, doors." He glanced at Tessa. "Plant."

Mandy frowned at the paper, and picked it up to study it. "Did you get anything more? Like colors or textures?" she asked Tessa.

"Not really. Except the floor is wood. Something pale, like maple, maybe, or washed pine. And the couch and chair are striped blue and white."

"And there's a dragon plant by the kitchen door and a big rubber plant in the corner."

Tessa blinked at her. "It was at night, so the corners were dark, but I had an impression of something big. It could have been a rubber plant."

"How the hell do you know about the plants?" Jay demanded.

Mandy rolled her eyes. "Because I put them there, silly. Honestly, Jay, where is your head? This drawing—" she waved the paper at him "—is my living room. They're at my beach house in Santa Rita."

JAY SLAPPED HIS FOREHEAD while Griffin gaped at Mandy. In Santa Rita? "That's impossible," he said.

"What is?" Mandy asked. "That they're there, or that we didn't think of it before now?"

Griffin turned to Jay. He felt sick. How could he have been such an idiot? "You better just fire me now. I don't know how I overlooked the beach house. It should have been the first place I checked."

"Don't beat yourself up," Tessa said, and laid a hand on his arm. "I saw the motel sign, remember? All this time we've been thinking they're on the road. And don't forget, Michelle, the salon owner, said they'd taken off."

The light touch of her fingers burned his bare skin. He stepped away under the pretext of pacing the office. If he was moving, she couldn't pin him down and make him feel what he had felt yesterday—both times. He wouldn't be tempted to touch those bare legs or run his hands over the worn cotton of her concert T-shirt.

Under which, he noted with some disappointment, she was wearing a bra.

How was it possible to want her again and yet urgently need to escape all that soft, sensual warmth?

"I'm sure they did," Mandy put in. "How do these visions or dreams or whatever work? Are they in real time or is there some kind of delay and they get replayed in your head, like TiVo?"

"Both. Either." Tessa blew a long breath up through her bangs. "If I touch something that belongs to a person, it seems to connect me with them. Or if I'm in a place that meant a lot to them, like down on the beach, the residual emotion seems to affect me."

"So what did you touch that connected you with Tessa?" Mandy looked intrigued, like a scientist who has discovered a new kind of animal behavior.

Griffin knew she was sharp. Obviously she was a lot sharper than he was. Here he'd drawn the floor plan, wondering the whole time how this was going to narrow the field of possibilities, while completely missing the fact that it was a room in a house in which he'd set up the alarm system himself.

Clearly he was not going to get his Boy Scout badge for observation. This is what happened when you let a woman distract you. It melted the brain cells you needed to do your job.

Tessa shrugged. "It could have been anything in the cottage. It could have been that photo on the wall in the hallway."

Mandy fell silent, thinking. "What were you wearing at the time?"

"Wearing?"

"Yeah. Clothes."

Griffin looked from one to the other. What the hell difference did that make?

"Um, my flowered cotton pj's," Tessa said slowly. "And a sweater I picked up at the thrift shop for five bucks. It's my favorite. Blue cashmere."

"What?" Mandy leaned over. "Blue cashmere?"

"Uh-huh. Talk about a deal. It's cut like a sweatshirt but it's totally luxurious. A person would have to be crazy or desperate to give it away."

"Oh, my God." Mandy sat on the desk a little too heavily, and the lamp teetered and settled back onto its base. "Can you do me a favor and go and get it?"

Tessa shrugged again. "Sure. Be right back."

Griffin eyed his boss's wife. She looked a little pale, and her gaze was unfocused, as if she were looking deep into her memory and trying to bring something out. "What's going on?" he asked.

"I don't know. I think—no, I won't know for sure until I see it."

"What's the big deal about a stupid sweater?" Jay demanded crossly. "Why aren't we getting in a truck and going to Santa Rita? Have you guys completely lost your focus? Griffin? I'm not paying you to watch a fashion show, here."

"Jay, shut up," his wife told him, only half her attention on him. The other half was locked on the door, behind which they heard Tessa's flip-flops slapping on the Mexican tiles. In a moment she came in holding the blue sweater.

Jay shut up.

Griffin closed his eyes to block out the memory of Tessa's body wrapped in the soft, sensual fabric.

When Mandy said, "My God. I knew it," he opened them.

"Knew what? What's the deal with the sweater?" he asked.

Mandy took it from Tessa and held it up. "This is Christina's. It's a Stella McCartney. One of a kind. She donated it to a charity event I did this past spring." She took a breath. "Tessa, think. What happens when you put this sweater on?"

"You're right," Tessa breathed, looking into Mandy's eyes as if they were having a conversation above and beyond words.

"Right about what?" Jay walked around the desk and took the sweater out of Mandy's hands. He looked it up and down as if there were a message pinned inside it. "Dammit, you two, give me some answers, here!"

"I picked it up the weekend before I came down here," Tessa said in a tone of soft amazement. "And the very first time I put it on, I saw Christina tied up on the bed. That was what made me call you guys."

"So all this time—" Mandy began, and Tessa nodded.

"Yup. All this time I've had a connection to her in my suitcase and didn't even know it. I thought the visions were completely random. But they weren't. I see her every time I put on the sweater."

"The point is, what are we going to do with it?" Jay snapped. "If that really is her sweater, I want you in it 24/7, picking up whatever there is to pick up. Meanwhile, Griffin, why are you still here? Why aren't you warming up the truck so we can go to Santa Rita?"

"Jay, I don't think you should go." Mandy laid a restraining hand on her husband's arm.

"Why the hell not? This is my daughter we're talking about."

"If she is there, do you think she's going to come out and talk to you when you're like this? I don't think so."

Bless Mandy. The thought of a half hour cooped up in a truck with a simmering volcano like Jay Singleton would have been torture.

"Let me go. I'm not exactly as threatening as you are." Mandy smiled at Jay, and the angry color started to recede from his face.

"Fine. Griffin will go with you."

"Um, Mandy, with all due respect, I think it should be me," Tessa said. "If I have the sweater on and circumstances change, chances are better that I might be able to pick up on it. Plus if she sees someone who doesn't have parental connections in her mind, she might be more inclined to listen to us."

Jay chewed his lip and glanced from one woman to the other. Two women who, in Griffin's mind, shared nothing but a similar hair color and an amazing intellect that seemed to click into high gear when they were together. Jay should be damned grateful they were batting for his side. But that didn't mean he wanted to be cooped up in that truck with Tessa, either. Even Jay by himself would be preferable to that.

Don't listen to her. He focused on the middle of Jay's forehead and sent a silent command. *Mandy should go. Mandy. Mandy.*

"All right. Griffin and Tessa," Jay finally said, and Griffin felt his gut sink. "But I want to be updated the minute you see her."

"Sure."

Shit.

18

"SO, WHERE'S THE BEACH HOUSE?" Tessa tossed her purse onto the seat and climbed into the truck. She'd barely restrained herself from doing the happy dance in Jay's office when he'd agreed with her about who was going on this little jaunt. A couple of hours alone with Griffin should turn him around; after all, a guy could only run for so long before he came back to where he started.

"At the beach." He wheeled the truck out onto the highway with a little more weight on the accelerator than was strictly necessary, given the lack of traffic.

Okay. So he was going to do this the hard way.

"At the low-rent end, where the canneries are, or at the high-rent end, where you can buy a mailbox and maybe a shrub for half a million?"

"What do you think?"

Tessa had always thought sex was supposed to make you happy and relaxed. Maybe someone should tell that to Mr. Grumpy, here. Or maybe he was still feeling embarrassed for having overlooked an obvious love nest while he was chasing around after bouncers, hairdressers and executives' houses.

"Well, that depends." She kept her tone light and oblivious. "If the house was in the prenup and Mandy owned it before she married Jay, then I would say it would be in the middle, maybe with a view of the cannery end but not actually there. If they bought it after the wedding, then of course it would be at the other end. Possibly with a couple of acres and maybe a yacht parked at the bottom of the garden."

"Yachts are moored. And she owned it before she met him."

"Aha. Why doesn't she have it rented? How come it's standing empty, waiting for teenaged girls to use it for a love nest?"

Griffin slanted a glance at her, then returned his gaze to the highway. "Do the Singletons strike you as the type to need the rental income?"

"They strike me as the type to leave no method of making money unturned."

He huffed a short breath that Tessa assumed was the hardboiled guy's way of indicating laughter. Geesh. She'd thought they were *so* past this. She wanted back the guy who fantasized about what her breasts looked like.

Hmm.

She'd changed out of her purple concert T-shirt before they left and, obeying orders, had pulled on Christina's blue sweater. But, with a shameless ulterior motive, she'd replaced the T-shirt with a bra that was nearly sheer and a sleeveless gauze top that not only turned transparent in the right light, but fastened with three strategically placed bows down the front instead of buttons. It made her look like a bad girl in virgin's clothing. She'd caught a client once leaning sideways, trying to see skin between the bows. Maybe it would have the same effect on Griffin.

She pulled the sweater off over her head and straightened her spine. A girl had to be aware of good posture at all times. Plus it really made the bows pop.

"We should talk about what we'll say to Chris—" Griffin glanced at her and stopped, his mouth hanging open on the forgotten word.

"Look out!" Tessa grabbed the wheel. The truck swerved toward the shoulder, Griffin grabbed it back and they sailed the other way, into the fast lane. He swore and corrected, settling into the middle of the right lane once more.

The corners of Tessa's lips twitched. *Tessa one. Griffin zero.* "You were saying?" she asked sweetly.

His struggle to get the defensive shields back up was practically visible. "I was saying that we need to figure out how we're going to convince Christina to come home."

"I don't think we should."

He stared at her, then jerked his gaze back to the road as if it wasn't safe to look at her. Which, at the moment, it probably wasn't.

"What are you talking about? That's what we're being paid for."

She turned toward him in the seat, offering him a frontal view of the bows, and bit her lip, trying not to smile when he kept his gaze resolutely on the highway ahead. It wasn't that she didn't appreciate his desire to avoid a traffic accident. She just hoped his peripheral vision was good.

"She's eighteen, Griffin. She's making choices on her own. Maybe not the greatest ones, but she's in love. Her brain is malfunctioning."

"Yeah, no kidding."

She hadn't meant it seriously, but it seemed he was determined to consider any form of attraction a malfunction. Her task today was clear.

"I think we should just let her know that Jay and Mandy are deeply concerned and would appreciate a phone call. If she's in no physical danger, we should leave it at that. Strong-arm tactics are just going to alienate her and dump us in her dad's camp, if we're not there already."

"I disagree. Jay sent me up here to bring her home, and that's what I'm going to do."

"Are you going to bind and gag the poor girl?"

"If that's what it takes."

"Ooh," she said, her tone soft and teasing. "How exciting. Do you carry cuffs?"

Another glare flashed across the width of the cab like lightning. "I'm being serious. Stop turning everything into a joke."

"I don't consider cuffs a joke. Not at all."

"Stop it. We agreed. This is inappropriate."

They turned off the highway and took the avenue to the beach, which was shaded by tall palms that leaned over the road. All very picturesque, but she'd bet the town council worried about their tendency to send heavy fronds crashing down on unwary passersby.

"You might have agreed, but I didn't. Besides, how could it be inappropriate after last night?" she asked.

"Last night is not going to happen again."

En garde. Don't be too sure about that. "That would be a shame. I haven't had an orgasm like that in months. Somehow it's just not the same by myself."

His eyes widened a little at what she suspected he was seeing in his mind's eye. She bit her lip so she wouldn't grin.

"Okay," he said at last, "I have to admit, I haven't, either. But that doesn't make it right."

The King of Swords was good. Parry and riposte.

"It felt right," she suggested.

"Fortunately I don't base my definition of right on how it feels."

"Why not? When it comes to sex, it's a pretty good indicator."

"Not for me."

"What do you mean?"

But he flipped on his turn signal and turned onto one of the streets fronting the beach. "Here we are."

It was impossible to spar with someone who put up his sword and refused to play. But that was okay. She had all day for round two.

Mandy's beach house was not the ramshackle place that Tessa had imagined. A riot of dry-climate plants and shrubs crowded the path that led around to the front, facing the beach, and a couple of bushy dwarf cedars sheltered the door. The house was sided in scented redwood that had aged gracefully to silver by the action of wind and spray, and its trim was painted white. Above her, a dozen windows precisely shaped to form a huge trapezoid of light faced the ocean and made the view part of the living space.

Tessa couldn't even imagine the kind of rent a place like this would bring. Five grand a month?

The door was painted white, too. Griffin lifted a brass knocker shaped like an arched fish tail and let it fall a couple of times.

"No one's there," Tessa said. The place was empty, with none of the usual waves and currents of life that she could sense when there were people about.

"We'll wait a second. The bedrooms are in the back."

"There's no point. No one is here. Did you bring a key?"

But of course he had to go into cop mode and wait for the evidence of continuing silence to tell him there was no one home. She resisted the urge to roll her eyes. He pulled a key out of his pocket and let them both in, then tapped a number into the pad set on the wall inside the door to disable the alarm.

And there they were in the living room of her vision, complete with rubber plant and striped cushions on the couch in front of the window. A frieze of Greek keys had been painted on the walls just below the ceiling. She'd missed that in her vision, she supposed. She wandered into the kitchen, expecting to find coffee grounds in the coffeemaker, spoons in the sink, maybe a wadded-up paper napkin or two, but there was nothing.

She wasn't much of a cook, but even she could tell that Mandy had poured a whole bunch of money into this custom kitchen. The sinks were color-coordinated with the granite counters, and a huge copper oven hood covered the cooktop. Implements and a string of what Tessa hoped was fake garlic hung from a rack suspended from the ceiling. The place was so clean it practically squeaked.

Either the runaways were excellent housekeepers or her vision of them in the room behind her had been of a time other than last night.

She hoped she was wrong.

She followed Griffin down the hallway with its cool floors—maple, not washed pine—to the bedrooms. Man, what she wouldn't give to live in a place like this. Mandy had fabulous taste. The bedrooms were like something out of a Greek idyll, all blue and white with warm touches of peach and yellow in pillows and chairs. Two smaller bedrooms contained queen-size beds and pine dressers, and the friezes painted on the walls were of shells and seaweed. Then Griffin stopped in the doorway of the master bedroom.

A mermaid flipped her tail at them from a huge mural

painted on the wall behind the bed. Fish and kelp surrounded her in a joyous circle, and shells and starfish formed a garland at the bottom.

"Wow," Tessa said. "Who did that?"

"Mandy. There's one similar in her and Jay's bedroom. Some Greek goddess whose name I forget."

"Aphrodite?" Tessa guessed aloud. "Think Jay gets the hint?"

"He won't let her paint anywhere else, but I think she's getting ready to do something in the kitchen. He never goes in there, and she's been staring at the walls a lot lately."

Tessa had a feeling that Mandy would find a lot in common with Gaia Tillman, her footloose artist mother. And Jay was obviously pulling his control tactics again, the big philistine. Mandy should be able to paint wherever she pleased.

Of course, the mural over the bed brought one's attention to the bed, with its vast expanse of warm yellow coverlet on which squares of sunlight fell through the mosaic of shaped windows.

Griffin's attention fell on it at the same time.

Round two, she thought gleefully. Let the games begin.

Pretending to be searching for clues or whatever detectives did, she moved into the bedroom and made a show of looking into the empty walk-in closet.

"It doesn't look as if anyone has been here in a while," she said helpfully.

"I'm going to check around downstairs," Griffin said, and took a step back, away from the door.

"Oh, wait, what's this?" Deliberately, she moved into the path of the sunlight in front of the windows and gave him her body's profile under the pretext of checking the empty wastebasket.

He stepped back into the bedroom, looking mesmerized.

"Nope, nothing in the trash." She extended her arms over her head and stretched luxuriously. "Ooh, that sun feels so good." The bow that held her blouse together at nipple level popped erect as she put tension on the fabric.

Tessa let her arms fall. A huge pine table stood under the windows, piled with books, pillows, and a vase of sea grasses. She turned her back to him, both hands flat on the table, and lifted her face to the sun. She could feel an answering heat in the gaze that tracked down her body. When it reached her backside in its short denim skirt, she heard him suck in a breath.

Tessa two, Griffin zero.

SHE WAS DOING THIS on purpose—standing in the sun like some fertility goddess, wearing transparent clothes, looking so touchable and sexy it was guaranteed to drive any man totally insane. Her body was like a magnet, calling out to his and making promises he knew she would take pleasure in keeping. He'd managed to fight her for half a day, but there was only so much provocation a man could take.

He didn't care that they were in someone else's private home. He didn't care that Christina wasn't here. All his brain had room for was the way Tessa leaned on that table with her face raised to the sun, her back arched and her derriere tilted up, her whole body an invitation.

He moved up behind her and bracketed her waist with his hands. His steps had been quiet on the patterned throw rug, but she didn't even jump. She'd been waiting for him to make a move. This should have annoyed the hell out of him, and if he weren't in such a state of sexual deprivation and sensual disarray, he might have been. But right now all he heard was that irresistible question posed by her body.

The one he needed to answer as soon as possible.

"What are you doing to me?" The words seemed to come from somewhere deep inside him, not from his brain.

"What you want me to do," she murmured. "Touch me. I want your hands on me."

The fragile fabric under his hands was warm from her skin. He moved his feet a little and snugged her bottom against him so that he could look over her shoulder and drop a kiss just below her ear. Hot blood spilled into his erection as he pressed it against the back of her little skirt, and his jeans tightened as the bulge behind them grew.

"Where do you want my hands?" he whispered. He knew where he wanted them. Right on the twin shadows he could see through the gauzy material. The neckline plunged to a bow that tied between her breasts. He'd wanted to undo it ever since she'd taken off her sweater in the truck.

"Here." She took both his hands in hers and cupped them over her breasts so that her nipples poked at his palms through two layers of fabric. He bit back a groan that was half gratitude and half delirium. "I know what you like."

White Indian gauze crumpled under his fingers as he lifted and fondled her flesh, brushing his thumbs over her nipples just so he could feel how hard they had become. As he did so, his hips seemed to move of their own volition, grinding his hardness against her soft, peachy bottom.

"I have to do this." With infinite slowness, he pulled one of the ties that held her top together, and the bow released. The other two followed more quickly, and he palmed her breasts again. "This isn't much of a bra," he noted. It was about as sheer as a garment could get. "Your nipples show through your top."

Her chuckle was full of carnal knowledge. "Gosh, I'm so embarrassed."

"You should be." He undid the front clasp and her bra sprang apart. "It plays hell with my concentration."

"Depends what you're concentrating on." She turned her head to nuzzle the side of his neck.

"You," he managed, and filled his hands with her breasts. "God, you drive me nuts." She was firm and round and heavy and soft at the same time. His hands had never felt anything so good.

"Up on the table."

He turned her around and she hopped up to sit on the worktable, which was built a little higher than normal and had thick turned legs for stability. "Perfect."

She drove her fingers through his hair as he cupped a breast in one hand and settled his mouth on her nipple. When he ran his tongue around the circumference of the areola, she squirmed. "I like that."

He did, too. He pleasured the other breast, enjoying both the textures of areola and skin under his tongue and the whimpers of desire he could elicit from her throat with a nibble or tug.

When she reached out and ran her fingers down the bulging ache that was his cock, he jerked and groaned. "If you do that, I'll come."

She ignored him, as he knew she would, and traced his length through his jeans, her fingers confident and trailing helpless pleasure in their wake. His knees were going weak. He leaned both hands on the edge of the table on either side of her and took her mouth in a punishing kiss.

She met him with equal force, her tongue promising

pleasures that her fingers only hinted at, sliding up and down his with suggestive sensuality.

He broke the kiss, breathing hard. Her thighs gripped his hips and she undid the top button of his jeans. He lowered his mouth and kissed her more gently, running his tongue along her lower lip as she slid the zipper down its track and plunged her hand inside his jeans to cup him through his shorts.

"Take these off," she whispered.

He toed off his boots, and yanked down his jeans and shorts together. His erection strained toward her as she did some kind of shimmy with her shoulders that shrugged off top and bra, and made her breasts jiggle in a way that was completely feminine and the most erotic thing he could remember seeing in a long time.

As she tossed her little skirt and panties aside, he saw with a jolt that she had been wearing a thong. A red one. He could have run his hands up under her skirt at any time today and felt nothing but smooth apricot skin. But no, he'd been too busy trying to ward her off, trying not to notice what she clearly wanted him to notice. Had he been insane?

He could spend his whole life watching her wriggle out of her clothes. Griffin lost all track of resolution and time, and when she kissed him again, he simply offered her his mouth in total bliss.

19

TESSA HAD NOT KNOWN there could be pleasure like this, or a man so skilled in the secrets of a woman's body. His ex-wife, whatever her name was, had to have been crazy for leaving him. And thank God it hadn't been her fate to hook up with anyone until now, though she'd often been puzzled as to why the cards had always told her to wait.

Now she knew.

Griffin's mouth and hands and that hot light in his eyes as he watched her undress—those were the reasons.

He touched her the way some women touched priceless velvet—as though it were a sensuous experience just by it-self. His tongue laved the sensitive places under her ear, at her throat, and in the valley between her breasts, returning again and again to trace the shape of her. It was as if he was trying to memorize her for a day when she wouldn't be there.

Goose bumps tiptoed over her arms.

"Are you cold?" he whispered.

"Not a chance." Not with this fever of desire in her blood, this hunger deep inside that was only stoked every time he tasted her skin and left a trail of pleasure. She let it erase the brief thought from her mind. "But just to make sure, let's trade."

He smiled against her skin. "What, me on that table? I'd break it for sure."

She slid off the table and gave him a full-body kiss that must have made his knees go weak, because when it ended, he was half-leaning, half-sitting on the edge of it.

"Go on. All the way up on it," she commanded. With one hand, she reached for the pale pine office chair at one end, and seated herself in front of him, between his legs, as if she were going to—

"What am I, lunch?" His voice sounded husky with anticipation, and she grinned up at him.

"Absolutely."

The skin on the inner side of his thigh felt soft under her cheek, and the muscles quivered under her tongue. She tasted her way up his right thigh and turned left when she got to the top.

"I can't hold out much longer, sweetheart," he said gruffly. "I'm set to explode." His fingers were splayed on the tabletop as though he was trying to hold on to it and not slide off. His cock was rigid, standing straight out from his body, and when she took him in her mouth at last, he dragged air into his lungs in a gasp.

His flesh filled her mouth, and she circled the rim with her tongue, seeking the sensitive nerve endings that would bring him the most pleasure. Her busy tongue laved him the way he had pleasured her areolas, faster and faster.

When she felt his hand convulse in her hair, she slowed and made a questioning sound.

"Tess—now—"

He scooted back on the table, forgetting all about whether it would hold their weight or not, and when she scrambled up beside him he took her in his arms and rolled her on top of him. With infinite slowness, his solid heat entered her, smooth as satin, because she was already soaked with desire and the pleasure she took in tasting him.

"Oh, yeah," he grated. He drove his hips forward, clasping his hands around her waist and pulling her to him more tightly. She wrapped her legs around him and he made a sound of satisfaction. "That's it, Tess," he encouraged her. "Let me have all of you."

I wish that was what you wanted.

What?

She was so surprised by the sudden thought that her legs relaxed and she nearly lost her grip on his body.

His big hands gripped her hips and he groaned. "You are so tight. So slick. I love how you feel, inside and out." He thrust into her again and she abandoned thought, letting his body take her to that place where thought didn't exist, only sensation. His strokes filled her completely, excited her past bearing. And he was a man who could multitask. She arched toward him and he suckled one breast, adding a river of pleasure flowing between his mouth and her clitoris. Then he slipped one finger between the lips of her vulva and stroked her clit, and with that stroke she lost her mind—and her control.

She cried out as her orgasm blossomed like a hot, red flower deep inside her, tingling through every nerve, all the way out to her fingertips. She couldn't bear this much pleasure. She was going to pass out any second…

With a final thrust, Griffin gasped, grabbed her so they both could keep their balance, and spent himself inside her, his body pulsing with helpless pleasure. Trembling, she fell forward against him and he wrapped his arms around her, murmuring sounds that she couldn't quite hear but whose meaning was perfectly clear.

Still intimately joined, she rested against his chest, gasping a little as her breathing came back to normal. His heart pounded against hers and they stayed that way, in the peaceful aftermath of lovemaking, until their bodies quieted.

The cards had told her to wait, Tessa thought, her mind still flying halfway between the sky and the earthy reality of the tangle they made of legs and arms. What would they have to say now?

WHAT WOULD IT BE LIKE to have a woman like this around every single day?

Griffin pulled Tessa with him down to the carpet. Warm and pliant and exhausted, she lay curled next to him as though they had been together for years and always fit together like this after sex. Griffin closed his eyes and just enjoyed the hell out of the moment, before it disappeared.

Because the happy moments always did. No matter how hard he worked to keep them, they slipped through his fingers and dissolved like sugar in warm water, never to be seen again.

Sheryl had taught him many things, some of them good even, but her most enduring lesson had been learning not to trust what made you happy. And she'd never said a word on the subject. She'd been the kind to lead by example.

Was he going to let those lessons rule the rest of his life? Not allow himself to be happy? Of course not.

Then why was he punishing himself? Did he think that if he suffered enough, she'd come back to him? But he didn't want her back. Caleb was welcome to her—if he could hang on to her.

Then why not give Tessa a chance?

He opened his eyes and looked at the woman whose blond hair tumbled over his shoulder to silence the voice of his conscience.

"Hey," he said softly, "are you asleep?"

"No, I'm just lying here being happy," she murmured into his chest.

"Think we should move? Jay will be waiting to hear something."

"He can wait five minutes."

Griffin chuckled, and the shaking of his chest made her lift her head and smile in return. His body stirred again at the sight, a thing he would never have believed possible after what they'd just done on Mandy's worktable. But they couldn't afford the time for seconds. Not yet, at least.

To get his body and his brain back in working mode, he kept talking. "I thought you learned on your first day that that wasn't true."

"I also learned that you have to stake your territory right away with that man, or you'll never get it back." She looked over her shoulder, obviously a woman who could take a subtle hint. "Where did I put my clothes?" She rose to her knees, and he let her go with regret. While she hunted up her scattered garments, he straightened the books that had shifted on the worktable.

"I guess we'd better be at least as tidy as Christina and Trey."

"If they were even here," he said as he dressed swiftly.

"They were here." She tied the last of the bows on the front of her blouse and tightened it with a tug. "What I saw was in color and really vivid, like the first one I had of her. That means it was happening in real time. And it was happening here, contrary to the evidence. Or lack thereof."

Griffin wasn't about to argue with her and spoil the mood. He couldn't, anyway. What did he know about the way a sensitive saw things? All he knew on the subject was distilled from ancient episodes of *The X-Files* and from spending the last several days with her.

One thing for sure—it would take a lot of faith and flexibility to live with a woman like Tessa. Qualities he was a little short on these days.

With a final look around to make sure they had disturbed nothing else, he led the way out of the house and reset the alarm.

By the time they were back in the beat-up familiarity of his truck and rolling down the highway at a comfortable eighty miles an hour, he had begun to feel as if the whole morning had taken place in a dream. A house he hardly knew, pleasure he'd never known, a woman he couldn't imagine knowing…driving back to Jay's was like coming back to the real world.

And the real world, for all its faults and risks and dangers, was the only one in which he was comfortable. He knew nothing of Tessa's, with its visions and bright colors and cheery optimism. It was foreign, as different as Kansas was from Oz.

And there was nothing wrong with Kansas, thank you very much.

HE WAS DOING IT AGAIN. Tessa felt Griffin's emotional withdrawal like the slow leaching of light out of the day at twilight. She was a morning person herself. She loved light and possibility and the scent of hot coffee. Twilight, with the slow triumph of night, was the time of day she liked the least. Not even the sight of Venus glowing on the horizon could redeem the encroachment of night.

And now Griffin was going gently into his emotional good night, as Natalie had told her he did, just when she was really getting to like him in the brightness of day.

There had to be something she could do to break this pattern. Sex helped, but its effects didn't seem to be permanent. How was she going to create a change? Was it even possible?

When they got back to the Singleton estate, it was to find both Jay and Mandy gone. "*El Jefe* says for you to call him the minute you get back," Ramon's voice reported at the gate. "He's in some big shot meeting, so he says to text message him *Yes* if you found her and *No* if you didn't."

"Will do." Griffin leaned out the driver's window. "What about Mandy? I can give her the status, at least."

"She wanted to help with the detecting," Ramon told them. "She went to get a facial at someplace with a strange name."

Tessa leaned over, placing a hand on Griffin's thigh for balance. It did not help that the muscles in his leg jerked as if he'd been ambushed. Sigh.

"You mean Oraia?" she asked Ramon—er, the speaker box standing in for Ramon.

"Yeah, that was it. I feel sorry for the stylist who gets her. She used to be a lawyer, you know. Really good at the old cross-examination."

"Thanks, Ramon." The gate opened and Griffin drove through. "It's not likely she'll get much more out of Michelle than you did," he said to Tessa as he pulled the truck around to the back of the garage. "Plus she's the step-mother. If Michelle is on Christina's side she'll be more likely to put up a smoke screen and tell her they went to Vegas or something."

"We know they're not in Vegas." She climbed out of the truck and he joined her on the path.

"We know they weren't last night, if your vision was accurate. For all we know, they could be by now." He tapped his watch, as if to prove the point.

"It was accurate," she said stubbornly.

"So you said." His tone was mild but behind the words she heard *no proof* as clearly as if he'd said them.

A cloud passed over the late-afternoon sun. The last of her happy mood evaporated and suddenly she felt cross and frustrated. After all she'd done to prove herself to him, proving she wasn't a fraud and she had real help to offer— not to mention blowing his mind making love not thirty minutes ago—they were back at square one.

"I said it because it's true. Look, Griffin, are we going to go around and around about how accurate I am, or are you ever going to just trust me?"

"I do trust you."

She stopped on the warm salmon-colored flagstones of the patio between the house and the cottage. "You say that, but behind it your brain is asking for proof, demanding evidence that I don't have. Do you have any idea how difficult you're making this for me?"

"It's a difficult case."

Ooh, she just wanted to shake that calmness out of him. She wanted the hot, passionate man who'd taken her on a table.

"You're making it more difficult every time you say something that makes me doubt myself. I know what I see is true, but every time you second-guess me or go off to find something to back up what I say, it just makes it harder for me to trust myself. It's a circle, Griffin. Between you and me."

"There's nothing between you and me," he said a little too quickly.

"You don't even believe that yourself. What happened at Mandy's house wasn't *nothing*. You just won't let yourself believe it's something."

He stepped back, almost involuntarily, and in the air between them Tessa could swear she saw the flash of a sword. Or maybe it was just the sun, glinting off the windows. The King of Swords was doing his level best to fend her off, but she was too keyed up to let him get away with it.

"How do you know what I believe?" he asked, his tone rough with control.

"I read your mind," she snapped.

"Bullshit."

"Of course it's bullshit. Everything I say is bullshit until you do your little investigation and fact-check and come up with something to back me up. Except when it comes to emotions, Griffin. You've got no fingerprint kit there, have you? You've got nothing but instinct and your gut, and those failed you before, didn't they?"

"You don't know anything about me." His eyes narrowed.

"You'd be surprised what I know. About Sheryl. And Caleb. And what they did. But that was then, Griffin. This is now, six years later. This is you and me. And if there's—"

But she got no further. Whatever tenuous hold he had on his self-control snapped. "Don't you talk about her!" he roared. "My life is none of your goddamn nosy psychic business!"

He turned and power-walked around the side of the garage. In a moment the truck fired up with a roar that echoed his own, the distress of a caged creature who has grown used to its cage and can't tolerate the poking of the stick through the bars.

The truck accelerated up the driveway, and a cloud of exhaust drifted gently over the hedge between the patio and the drive. He didn't even slow down at the gate.

Smart Ramon. Evidently he had left it standing wide open.

Stupid Tessa. Why couldn't she learn to pick her moments better and keep her mouth shut? No wonder all her relationship prospects got frightened away.

Tessa pushed open the front door of the cottage and went in. The windows had been thrown open and the purple T-shirt she'd tossed on the bed had been hung up in the closet. There were new towels in the bathroom.

She dropped her purse on the computer table, slumped on the window seat and gazed absently at the view. Even though she was convinced she was right, she had hurt him with the mention of Sheryl. If he wouldn't let her make it up to him, it might take him a while to bandage his wounds and put his armor on again. It hadn't been fair to toss his ex-wife's name at him as if she'd read his mind when actually she'd done some fact-checking of her own. That was the next thing to a lie, and if he'd given her the chance, she would have admitted it. But they had both lost their tempers and now things were going to be awkward.

No, that was a lie, too. It was more than awkward.

She had hurt him and because of that, she hurt. And why did she hurt? Because she cared about his feelings.

Come on, it's more than that. The truth is, you care about him. Griffin Knox, the guy who makes you smile and want to wear see-through clothes. The guy who takes better care of his truck than he does of himself.

The guy who probably won't let you within touching distance ever again.

20

With a sigh, Tessa got her cell phone from her purse and came back to the window seat. She keyed in the first number on autodial, and when she got voice mail at Linn's office, dialed the second one.

Her sister answered on the second ring. "Oh, hey, Tessa."

"What are you doing home?"

"I pulled night shift this week. I have to go in about an hour."

"Kellan, too?"

"Nah. He's a corporal now. He gets dibs on days. But we manage to meet for supper. Except for tonight. We have to go pick a tux for him. But I bet you didn't call to talk about my shift or tuxes."

"No." The word was a disconsolate plea for help.

"Uh-oh. That sound means one of two things—either you got evicted or it's man trouble."

"The second."

"That's a relief. It's easier to find a man than it is to find a decent rent-controlled apartment. So, who is it? Surely you can't have met someone at Jay Singleton's holy of holies. Unless maybe you've got a thing for the chauffeur."

"He's, like, nineteen, so no. It's Griffin."

Silence breathed down the line. "Griffin."

"Yeah, you know. Fort Knox."

"You're having man trouble with Griffin Knox? Is that even possible?" Linn sounded a little winded.

"At the moment, nothing is possible with him. We had fabulous sex this afternoon on the table in Mandy Singleton's beach house and the next thing you know, he's shouting at me and roaring out of here in his truck."

"Sex. On a table. With Griffin Knox, who arrested you," Linn repeated, as if to make sure she'd heard correctly and they were talking about the same person.

"Yes. But Natalie Wong was right. He's not emotionally available. We enjoyed the heck out of each other and practically as soon as it was over, he was backing away, then walking away, then driving away at a high rate of speed." She sighed. "I just don't know what to do, Linn."

"My God. Tessa, have you fallen in love with that guy?"

Deep inside, Tessa felt a deep knell of confirmation, as if something she'd always needed to know had finally been answered.

This was it. This was why the cards had said to wait.

"I…I hope not," she said at last.

"I hope not, too. He's a one-way ticket to a broken heart, which has to be a line from a country western song somewhere."

"I don't listen to country western."

"Well, listen to your big sister, then. There can't be two people on the planet more different than you and Griffin. You were thrown together for a job, you had a little fun, now he's decided he can't handle it and it's over." Linn's voice softened. "Don't throw your heart away on him, honey. Natalie is right. She called and told me you were doing background on him, by the way, and I wondered what was up."

"Nothing's up, I guess. I thought I could open a door for him, but he's locked down tight."

"It happens," Linn said sympathetically. "Look at me and Jordan. Remember him? The pilot? I tried to open up his door for three years."

"Jordan was a jerk."

"I know, and if you've fallen for Griffin he must not be one, but sometimes you just have to know when to cut your losses."

Tessa supposed that was true, but the optimist in her always hoped that every problem had a solution. Some didn't. Maybe some problems just wanted to be left alone.

She said goodbye to Linn and put the phone back in her purse. If ever there was a time to consult the cards, it was now.

The Queen of Wands smiled at her from the front of the little velvet bag as she shook the cards into her hand. "I could use some help from you," Tessa told her. Then she sat on the rug in a long beam of sunshine and shuffled and cut, then chose one.

The Magician.

Tessa caught her breath. She should have consulted the cards before she'd called Linn and gotten all depressed. The Magician was her kind of card. He meant concentrating on what you wanted, committing to it, and then going after it. People often thought he pulled off miracles, but it was the power of his focus and simply doing what needed to be done that accomplished the seemingly impossible.

So there you were.

She needed to focus on doing what needed to be done, and that would help get her what she wanted. The seemingly impossible.

But what was that, exactly? Was it to return to her old life and focus on her thesis, so she could graduate—yep, that fell under "seemingly impossible"—and get on with the scary business of making a living?

Face it, Tessa, sensible people don't change their major four times. You stay in school because it's safe there. You don't actually have to get out and grow up and be useful. Or if not useful, then at least a benefit of some kind, helping people who need your skills.

And if she didn't want to focus on that, then how about the other impossible? How about Griffin?

Again, that deep sense of recognition sounded inside her, like the vibration of a bell that you can feel but not hear. Her instincts told her this was what she wanted, whether it was logical or practical or not. And Tessa had learned to listen to her instincts.

Her brain told her that Linn had all the facts right. But her heart and her internal sense told her that there was more to caring about someone than facts. There was action. There was sex. And there was opening up to one another and being honest.

Okay, so two out of three wasn't bad.

Through the open window, she heard the purr of a couple of very expensive engines, and then voices. Jay and Mandy were home.

Well, in the absence of Griffin, she was going to have to check in and add a report of some kind to the one-word text message she presumed Griffin had gotten around to sending once he'd slowed down.

She crossed the patio and went around to the front door, which was closest to Jay's office. But for once the inner sanctum was empty. It felt just like Jay, though—big and full of importance and stress. A hundred years and half a dozen owners from now, it would probably still feel that way.

Tessa followed the sound of voices down the hall to the kitchen, where it seemed Mandy was making Jay a snack. Big shot meetings must make a guy hungry.

"I told you, I don't know anything more than that one word—oh, Tessa." Jay put down his cheese-and-croissant sandwich and motioned for her to come in. "All I know from Griffin is 'no.' What does that mean? And where the hell is he?"

"It means no, she wasn't at the beach house this morning." Tessa pulled up a stool and sat opposite him at the huge butcher-block table. "And Griffin drove out of here about twenty minutes ago. I don't know where he went."

"Oh, I passed him when I was coming back from Santa Rita," Mandy told him. "I got him on the walkie-talkie. He's on his way back."

That wasn't enough time for a guy to cool off and find his equilibrium. Tessa wished Mandy's timing had been off just a little so that they might have missed each other. Or that the battery had gone dead in her phone. It was hard to prepare herself to talk to him when she had no idea what frame of mind he'd be in.

"Well, you can tell us as well as he can," Jay said, chomping into his sandwich. "Start at the top. Don't leave anything out."

Yeah, right. She started at the top and left whole paragraphs of things out. And by the time she got to the end, Griffin was leaning on the kitchen doorjamb, arms crossed over his chest and his gaze fixed on her. She lost her train of thought and stumbled to a halt.

"Can you add anything to that, Griffin?" Jay asked.

"Just a few opinions."

"Let's hear 'em."

"Why doesn't Mandy update us first?" Griffin suggested.

"Come on in and sit." Mandy waved him to a stool next to Tessa, but he took the one on the end instead. Mandy shrugged and brought her own croissant to the table, taking the stool he had rejected.

He won't sit next to me. Not a good sign.

Mandy took a fortifying nibble of her sandwich. "I went to Oraia to get a facial and see what I could learn." She glanced at Tessa. "They do a great facial. You should go there. Ask for Bonita."

"But did you talk to Michelle?" Griffin wanted to know. "She's the one who said Christina and Trey had plans to go away."

"Well, that's the funny thing." Mandy took another bite. "Bonita doesn't know Trey or Christina. I guess she's new. But what she does know is that Michelle hasn't been in the shop for two weeks. Apparently she's on vacation, diving in the Catalinas."

"What?" Griffin looked blank.

"That's impossible." Tessa stared from Jay to Mandy and back. "She must have come back."

"Not according to Bonita. I asked around. No one has seen her since the day she left."

"Which one of you talked to her?" Jay demanded, glaring at Griffin.

"I did," Tessa said, and the glare turned on her like a bad-tempered searchlight. "I pretended I was Christina's friend Ashley."

"Was Griffin with you?"

"Of course he was. He's been with me every waking hour since I got here, per your orders."

Don't lose your temper. Up until now she hardly knew

she had a temper. But there was something about these men that just rubbed her the wrong way. Separately, she could deal with them. Together? Bad news.

Jay looked at Griffin. "And you believe she talked to this Michelle."

Griffin nodded. "At the time, I did."

"What do you mean, 'at the time'?" Tessa demanded. "You were sitting right there. We called early, so she was there before the shop opened and people saw her. And then we went and looked Trey up at Stellar Memory. That's how we found him."

"It couldn't have been her," Mandy observed. "The Catalinas are a long way from here."

"It doesn't matter whether it was or not," Tessa said. "The point is, we got the name we needed. We found out who Christina's boyfriend is."

"For all the good that did us," Griffin put in. "Let's just say it wasn't Michelle who answered the phone. Who could it have been? Someone who figured out you were playing games and decided to play one of her own? Trey's name is all over the papers in this neck of the woods. Maybe this person saw it and decided to pull your leg right back."

"It was Michelle!"

"But how do you know?" Jay asked.

"That's the point!" Tessa's frustration increased. "I *did* know. It was Michelle Oraia, who owns the shop. I sensed it."

"Just like you sensed they were at the beach house last night?" Jay said, and looked to Griffin for confirmation.

He shook his head. "There was no evidence at all that they were there. No trash, no damp in the shower, nothing."

"She said that they were very neat." Jay put his sandwich down. "I didn't know she meant so neat they weren't even there."

"They were there," Tessa said, but even as the words came out of her mouth, she knew it was pointless. "I saw them there, last night. I just don't know where they are now. I need to go and get the blue sweater and find somewhere quiet, so I can—"

"That won't be necessary." Jay's tone was flat.

Tessa glanced at Mandy, but her face was as smooth as it probably was in the courtroom, right before she made her closing argument. No help there.

Griffin? With her eyes, she appealed to him to help her out. He had believed her when she'd called Michelle before. And they had identified Trey together. The guy was in the Christmas party picture. Why was Griffin doing this?

"Thank you for your time, Tessa," Jay said. "But I believe we've been a little misled."

"I haven't misled you! In fact, I've—"

"I didn't say it was you who misled us. Though these discrepancies between your visions and reality are a little disturbing. I think now that it's time we pursued a more— shall we say, realistic line of investigation."

"But it is real!"

"I'm going to disagree with you."

"We're not sure how you define *real*." Mandy smiled, as if to indicate that these were the facts, but she wasn't holding them against Tessa. "In the beginning Jay and I agreed to overlook this business about Griffin's arresting you for fraud. But since we don't seem to be seeing any results, here, I'm feeling very uneasy about you working with us."

Tessa felt as if she'd been thrown to the ground. She

tried to drag a breath into her lungs that were suddenly having trouble working. "Remember that I was not convicted, or even charged." One breath. Good. Try another. Now, talk. "He arrested me by mistake. You can ask him."

Jay waved an arm, as if to get their attention. "Arrested, charged, it's all the same to me. The point is, we need to try something else. While you're packing up your things, I'll be in my office writing you a check. I'll meet you there in, say, ten minutes." Jay pushed himself back from the table with an air of finality.

"Mr. Singleton, it's you who's making a mistake now," Tessa said desperately. "We're only half a day behind Christina. If you'd just let me—"

"Ten minutes, Tessa," he said from the doorway. "And I suggest that this time, you don't keep me waiting."

21

I don't know which is worse—fear or disappointment. With fear, at least there's the hope that everything will turn out okay. But with disappointment that hope gets killed and you're left with nothing.

So here I stand with nothing. Less than nothing, in fact. Because I insisted on racing down rabbit holes with this psychic, any trail Christina might have left is stone cold. I should have listened to Griffin. I should have called Barbara right away and asked for her help, because God knows Christina could have jumped on a plane and gone back to Boston.

Should have, could have, would have. The most useless words in the English language. They mean failure.

No, come on. What's failed here is me. The whole reason I wouldn't let Griffin call in the police is because I was afraid of losing Christina. I was afraid Barbara would convince her to go away—but if my little girl really wanted to stay here, nothing would have made her go back, not even Barbara.

And now I've really lost her. No matter what I did or didn't do, she still chose Trey Ludovic and left me anyway. When am I going to get the opportunity to make this right?

Is it really too late? Am I going to lose my girl before I've had a real chance to be her father?

Father, ha. What kind of father am I?

I'm a joke as a father. The fact is, I chose work over my family and now I'm paying the price when my family chooses something else over me. Christina's no dummy. I taught her well that family isn't important. I taught her that if you chase something hard enough, you'll get it. She chased Trey Ludovic and got him, much as that sticks in my gullet.

Face it, Jay.

You brought this on yourself. The person to blame is not Barbara, not Tessa, not Griffin. The person to blame is you.

TESSA'S FACE HAUNTED GRIFFIN.

She had stared at Jay like a child on Christmas morning who has just had all her presents torn from her hands and given to someone else. No, it was worse than that. It was the face of a woman who has believed the best despite all odds, and who has just realized the worst has been waiting to ambush her all along.

Griffin shook off the memory of those eyes and the plea for support that had faded to pain and disappointment. It was true he had been of two minds about the information she'd given them. How much of their progress had come from her gift and how much was sheer coincidence and investigative luck?

It was too late now to debate it. He had his boss's runaway daughter to find.

His first call after the sound of the Mustang's perfectly tuned engine had faded out of his life was to the local P.D. to report Christina missing. Normally there would be a twenty-four-hour waiting period for a report to be filed after such a call, but when he'd explained that had expired long ago and told the duty officer just who was missing, a detective was dispatched within the hour.

The detective who now sat across the desk from Jay Singleton in the chair that Tessa had refused that first day. The woman's badge said her surname was Petrie, and her dark hair was cropped short in a no-nonsense style. She opened her notebook and took a pen from an enormous handbag that rested against the leg of the chair. It probably contained her handgun, a sack lunch and the policy and procedures manual.

"So, you've been investigating your daughter's disappearance privately?" she asked.

Jay nodded.

"Let me just say that after the first twenty-four hours the trail is often cold. Your first call should have been to us."

"I've called you now," Jay said shortly. "There has been no ransom note or any real indication she was kidnapped. One possibility is that she ran off with Trey Ludovic, who is—"

"I know who Trey Ludovic is. Stellar Memory, right?"

"The same."

"But he's got to be—" Detective Petrie stopped herself before she said "as old as you are" but Jay glared at her as if she had.

"Right." The woman scribbled in her notebook. "You know that technically she's not a child. In the eyes of the law, after the age of seventeen she can go where she wants with whom she wants, and there's not much our department can do about it."

Jay's eyes narrowed. "You can help us find her before

something happens, like they run off to Vegas and get married."

"This is a family matter, Mr. Singleton, not a crime."

"Do you investigate missing persons or not?" Jay had finally reached the end of his patience. "Do you have any idea how much I contributed to your department's last charity gig? I expect a little service in return."

The woman paled and Griffin leaned a shoulder on the window and looked out at the endless, monotonous crash of the breakers.

"I didn't say I wouldn't make some inquiries, in the interests of the community. But demands on our time are high. I just want to set your expectations."

"No, let me set yours. I want my daughter found, and I want her found now, otherwise your chief's pet charity had better not count on another cent from me. Is that clear?"

It was evidently common knowledge at the department just how big Jay's contribution to the policemen's community fund was. "I'll do what I can," Petrie finally said. "Where was she last seen?"

"At her cottage here on the property," Jay replied.

"Physically." Griffin's conscience prodded him again with the memory of Tessa's face. "We also had information she was recently at Mrs. Singleton's beach house." The detective was going to have to know why they'd waited so long to call her in. There was no point in putting it off.

Jay glared at him. "We've been using a psychic," he explained, then waved the idea away with one hand as Petrie's eyes popped with disbelief. "But it didn't work out. She saw Christina at my wife's beach house in Santa Rita last night in a vision. But when Knox here investigated, there was no evidence they'd been there. So I fired her."

"A good decision," Petrie agreed faintly.

Something in Griffin's gut gave him the figurative elbow. Or maybe it was his sense of fairness. He hadn't been fair with Tessa and her departure was his reward for that. "Most of her information was backed up with evidence," he said, "but I guess you can expect the universe to fire a blank now and then."

"I guess it was pretty stupid to waste valuable days on a psychic's babbling," Petrie snapped. "What were you thinking?"

"We were thinking that we didn't want this to be public knowledge," Jay said. "If you bring in the cops you're guaranteed to bring in the news vans."

"Not in this case." Petrie closed her notebook. "All I need is for it to get out that I'm cleaning up after a psychic."

Griffin frowned and decided that, if he had been the detective, he wouldn't be haranguing the family about their very real concerns. Or about their methods. After all, what was he, chopped liver? He'd been running the show up until now. He and Tessa had done the best they could with the limited tools they had at hand.

He had to face it. He almost had it wrapped. If he'd opened his mouth and backed her up instead of letting Jay crucify her with sarcasm and anger, he'd be this many hours closer to succeeding. If he'd said one word in her defense, he could have built up Jay's confidence in her, and he and Tessa would probably not only have found Christina, they'd be sharing a bed tonight.

Right, that's just what I need.

Of course it was. And now he'd put the kibosh on it for good. He was never going to see her again.

The chill of loss filled his gut as he acknowledged the truth of that. He tried to shake it off as he showed Petrie to the door. She paused on the steps outside.

"Former law enforcement?" she asked, looking him up and down with a tad more than professional interest.

He nodded, and she smiled. "I can always tell. What department?"

"Santa Rita P.D. Invalided out. Took a round in the knee."

"Ah." Her voice held sympathy. "Still, can't be a bad gig, working for Singleton. Though this whole psychic thing is a bit irrational. I'm surprised you allowed it."

"She was good." He could be as abrupt as Jay.

Petrie's gaze became flirtatious. "Maybe you can educate me. Bring me up to date. Say, over a drink down at the Pelican?" The Thirsty Pelican was a cop hangout close to the municipal pier. Griffin had gone there a lot after Sheryl. After he'd regained the ability to drive.

"No," he said. "But thanks. I have your card. I'll send you a briefing by e-mail so you have everything documented."

Detective Petrie withdrew visibly into "sexless police officer" mode. "Right. Meanwhile, I'll try to convince my lieutenant we should get a team down to that cottage to process it."

"Don't waste your time. I'd suggest the beach house in Santa Rita."

Petrie shook her head. "Not our county."

"So what? They'll assist you."

"Not for a missing person, especially if she's not a minor and there's no evidence of a crime. Like I said, I can make inquiries, check phone records, but no more. Unless evidence turns up that she actually has been kidnapped. Even then, you'd have to go to the Feds or CLEU."

CLEU.

What were the odds that Tessa would already have

called her sister about her firing? How close were they? Could Linn Nichols help?

Probably not more than she already had, with the under-the-counter phone records. And Linn would be least likely of all to put the state's resources to work for him if she knew he'd just helped to publicly humiliate her sister.

Look what had happened the last time he'd done that.

Griffin watched Detective Petrie drive off with a sense of relief. Then he walked around the back of the garage and climbed into his own truck. All he needed was a couple of hours away from here to clear his head, and then he'd get back on the case. He'd drive over to the beach house and go over it with a fine-tooth comb, without the beautiful distraction who might have made him miss something before.

He signaled and pulled onto the highway northbound to Santa Rita. If it hadn't been for Tessa, he'd probably have taken the good detective up on her offer of a drink and let nature take its course afterward. He'd have spent some time with her and then dropped out of her life, which had become his modus operandi for the past year or two. It was convenient, it was easy, and he didn't have to engage the drive belt that connected his libido and his emotions.

His emotions had engaged with a vengeance when Tessa had looked at him in the kitchen. He'd been so stunned by the collision between his need to keep his employer happy and his need to fold her in his arms and protect her from Jay's anger that he'd just stood there, immobilized, and watched the trust and hope drain out of her when he didn't step up to support her. His heart squeezed with pain in direct proportion to the pain he had caused her.

When he'd received his shield and gun, he'd vowed silently that he'd uphold the truth and believe in "innocent until proven guilty." That he'd fight on the side of the underdog. That he'd do the right thing, no matter what it cost him.

He'd learned soon enough that police work didn't lend itself to the first three in a lot of cases, so the shine had been rubbed off a lot of his youthful illusions pretty damn quick. But he still believed in the last one. It wasn't easy doing the right thing sometimes. In fact, even knowing what the right thing was could be hard, especially when you were facedown in a filthy corridor with a hysterical crackhead waving a Walther at you.

But he hadn't done the right thing by Tessa. Of course he had checked out everything she'd said because that was his job. However he should have told Jay that this wasn't because he didn't trust her, but because it increasingly proved that her visions were accurate.

With a sigh, he pulled into his driveway. His little house stood baking on its lot, the shutters closed against the sun so that it looked as if it were sleeping. Just like him. Pretending to be asleep, pretending to be unavailable, so no one would be tempted to knock on the door and make him feel again.

Frowning at his thoughts, he collected the mail from the box and let himself inside. He was by nature a methodical, neat kind of guy who didn't like a lot of stuff around, but what he had was always in its place where he could find it in a hurry. But the house felt even more spare and empty than it usually did. He had gotten used to Tessa's sunny presence with him, and now that it wasn't around, everything just looked dark and solitary.

He pushed open the drapes and opened a few windows.

An unopened soda was hiding in the back of the fridge, behind a rock-hard chunk of cheese. Popping the top, he took it into the backyard and, out of habit, looked over at the banana tree.

Uh-oh.

The damn tree, which had been growing despite his best efforts to ignore it, drooped disconsolately, its broad, serrated leaves turning jaundiced. "Aw, come on." He didn't care about the tree. But at the same time, he didn't want to see anything die on his watch, either. He dragged the hose over to it and soaked the ground. "Don't die on me now, you stupid thing. You've stayed alive to spite me so far."

The tree didn't answer, but the water disappeared into the hard ground with a sound like a hiss of relief. He stood there, hosing it down and sipping the soda, until water puddled at his feet. Then he hosed the tree's leaves for good measure.

The action of attempting resuscitation seemed to spark the need for activity. He turned off the water and went back in the house. Petrie's business card was still in his back pocket. With a sense that he needed to help set things right again, he flipped open his cell phone and punched in her number.

THE ONLY THING different in the apartment was the pile of mail, which had grown, and the plants, which had not. Yesterday all Tessa had managed to accomplish was to haul a load of laundry down to the communal laundry room and bring it up again when it was done. Today she filled the watering can and attempted to bring the plants back to life. She should have had someone come in to look after them. But she'd left in such a hurry, so excited to have a job and someone to believe in her, that she hadn't even thought about mundane things like what would happen to the African violet and the tray of herbs over the sink while she was gone.

They looked the way she felt: drab and droopy and lifeless. And while a drink of water might go a long way to fixing their problems, it wouldn't do much for hers.

Once her few plants were taken care of, she picked through the mail, but there was nothing in there but bills, ads, and offers for credit cards it would be fatal to her skinny bank account to use. Her next-door neighbor had dropped his used copy of this week's *San Francisco Inside Out* into her slot, which he did about once a week. She flipped its pages idly, pausing to read "Lorelei on the Loose," a column that was usually amusing but today just didn't interest her. It was about rich people who were famous for just that—being rich.

Yawn.

Then a photograph caught her eye at the bottom of the column, under a subhead that read "Trying to be Paris Hilton?" She blinked and looked closer. Under a neon sign that clearly read New York, New York, one of the biggest new casinos in Reno, patrons leaned over gaming tables. And there, front and center, were Christina and Trey Ludovic, photographed in the act of tossing the dice. Christina was laughing, and Trey, who hadn't photographed as well as he had in the Christmas party picture, was looking every bit the middle-aged executive. Including the harassed expression and the unsmiling mouth.

Tessa studied him for a moment. Something was bugging the guy, but what? The photographer? Worried that Daddy would read the paper and hunt him down like the dog he was? Her gaze dropped to the caption.

"Last night at NY squared, who should storm the tables but rich girl Christina Singleton, on the arm of a guy both declined to name. Paris waited till she was twenty-one before she burst on the club scene. Christina's obviously warming up with her companion's luck at the Reno casinos."

That was why they hadn't been at the beach house the day before yesterday, Tessa realized with sudden certainty. They'd gone to Reno. The question was, why? To pay their "Nevada taxes" at the slot machines? Or for another reason—one that involved drive-through chapels and ministers in spandex who sang "Love Me Tender" on request?

She glanced around wildly. The sweater. What had she done with Christina's cashmere sweatshirt? Her feet slipped on the bare wood of the floor as she dashed into the bedroom, where the pile of clean laundry still sat in its basket. Undies, tops, dress, shorts—aha.

She tossed the sweater in the air and yanked it over her head.

Come on, universe. Give me a sign. Do I jump in the car and redline the speedometer over the Sierra Nevada mountains, or have they hopped a plane already and begun a honeymoon in Tahiti?

Nothing happened.

Okay. That was okay. She should just go about her normal business and sooner or later something would come to her. It always had before. She just needed to be patient.

But somehow the sense of urgency inside her increased. She couldn't sit still. Instead, she found herself walking around the apartment, doing stretches, picking things up and putting them down again, all the time feeling as though time was ticking away and she was going to miss it.

She had no idea what "it" even was. A plane? An opportunity? What?

A door slammed and she whirled away from it.

The blue-and-white-striped couch in front of the window with its ocean view looked soft and inviting, and she watched Christina drop onto it. The girl craved the embrace of something, even upholstery. Trey had left and he wasn't coming back. The cotton covering the cheery yellow pillow soon became soaked with her tears. Before long she needed a tissue. Her thoughts sounded in Tessa's mind. So what if they found something in the wastebasket. Trey was just being paranoid about leaving no traces. Mandy would understand that she just needed a little time here where it was quiet, where no one would ask questions. Where she could be alone to lick her wounds.

Alone!

Christina wailed and buried her face in the wet pillow. How was she going to face the rest of her life alone?

Tessa came back to herself as suddenly as she'd left, sitting on a kitchen chair with her head buried in her arms and no memory of how she got there. She blinked and lifted her head, then patted herself to make sure her flesh and the sweater were real.

Christina was back at the beach house. Tessa now knew the source of the feeling of urgency in her gut. She had to get down there before the girl decided to do something drastic or dangerous to herself. In her present frame of mind, freshly dumped and vulnerable, Christina might think a reasonable solution would be to go to a club and hit on the nearest male over thirty. Or she might call up her girlfriends and decide a cross-country trip back to Boston was the answer. In either case, the results could be disastrous.

22

TESSA YANKED a few clean clothes out of the laundry basket and stuffed them into her striped beach carryall. "Be good," she told the African violet, then ran out of the apartment and took a bus to the garage where the Mustang was stored. She was negotiating traffic on the Highway 101 interchange when her cell phone rang.

Linn, wanting to talk about fabric swatches.

Jay, wanting to rehire her.

Griffin, wanting to apologize for leaving her swinging in the wind.

But it was none of the above. For once, her intuition had failed her.

"This is Detective Petrie from the sheriff's office," a woman's voice said crisply. "I understand you've recently been employed by Jay Singleton to help find his daughter."

"Yes." She certainly hadn't seen *that* one coming.

"In what capacity?"

"I'm a sensitive." Tessa put the phone between her ear and shoulder, changed up into fourth gear and accelerated off the cloverleaf and onto the freeway. "I've been working with Griffin Knox, trying to trace Christina using psychometry and dream work."

"Uh-huh." The woman's voice was flat with skepticism. Even with the wind in her ears from having the top down, Tessa could hear it.

"What can I do for you, Detective?" she asked, forcing herself to be patient. For all she knew, a person could be arrested for contempt of law enforcement officers.

"Speaking of Griffin, I had a little chat with him yesterday. He suggested that I call you."

Yesterday? And it had taken this long for her to get around to it? "Did something happen?"

"No, not to my knowledge. Why do you say that?"

"I just wondered. Because Griffin doesn't believe in what I do. He has no reason to ask you to call me unless something happened."

"I'll have to disagree with you there. We agreed that he'd brief me on this case, but he suggested that the most efficient way to do that would be for you to talk to me."

"He did?" Tessa's brain jogged along in first gear, trying to close the gap between the guy who'd fed her to Jay Singleton and this new guy who thought she had something to contribute. Or rather, the old guy of a couple of days ago who had worked with her and thought she was real.

She couldn't figure it out, and gave up. Detective Petrie was talking again, anyway.

"He gave me some details that helped me map out their trail, and a list of Christina's friends so we could collect phone records."

"We already did that."

Detective Petrie paused. "Maybe you did, but let me do the detecting now, okay? It is, after all, my job."

"Uh, okay. You'll find a lot of calls to Oraia, a salon Christina goes to. She's friends with the owner, Michelle, who apparently has been out of town for two weeks." *Ex-*

cept for one day, when she happened to be in the shop and talked to me.

"What about her hangouts, places she and her friends go?"

"They dance at Atlantis a lot. But we already went there, too. We were supposed to show her picture to the bouncers to see if they could identify Trey, but we already found out who Trey was through Michelle."

"Bouncers," Petrie said slowly, sounding as if she were writing it down.

"Detective, you don't need to waste your time on all this. Christina is at Mandy's beach house."

"Yes, apparently you already said that."

"No, not the other day. Today. Now."

"And how do you know this?"

"I just saw her. In a vision. Trey just dumped her and she's there all alone. Somebody needs to go and get her before she does something stupid."

"You saw her in a vision."

"Yes!" Was the woman deaf or had her cell phone cut out during all of that? "Did you hear what I said?"

"Oh, yeah, I heard it. But Griffin Knox says that house is empty and has been for some time. I'm not about to go chasing off up the coast on the basis of a dream when there's real legwork to be done."

"But we already *did* the—"

"I don't know what he was thinking. I was expecting real information. Uh, thanks for your time, Ms. Nichols."

"Wait—" But the dial tone was already buzzing monotonously in her ear.

Tessa snapped the phone shut with a flick of her wrist and tossed it in her carryall.

Stupid woman. Why did she bother with cops of any description, anyway? She could do this herself. She'd drag Christina home kicking and screaming if she had to. She'd show these people who had skills and who didn't.

Tessa put her foot to the floor and the Mustang leaped forward with a joyful roar.

DETECTIVE PETRIE seemed to think that Tessa was their personal private joke.

"...so then she tells me that our girl is back at the beach house, like I'm going to jump right in the car and hustle over there. I tell you, Griffin, you have my sympathy. I'm not sure how many peace officers would be able to handle Jay Singleton forcing them to work with a psychic. I mean, try to set foot in the Pelican once *that* gets around."

Cell phone to his ear, Griffin leaned on his sliding glass door and gazed out at the banana tree. Was it his imagination, or had the thing perked up a little? "She called with information and at the time, we—"

But Petrie interrupted. "So look, I'm going to go talk with the owner down at the Atlantis. We'll see how forthcoming he is when he gets a badge flashed in his face."

If she wanted to chase her tail following up empty leads, that was fine by him. Anything to get her out of his way. "Okay."

It was his own fault that she felt free enough to talk about Tessa like this. All he'd had to do when she'd come over to Jay's was make it clear that Tessa had been helpful to the case. Then her attitude might have had, if not admiration, then at least not this smiling, elbow-in-the-ribs derision. But he had not stood up for Tessa. Once again, he'd withdrawn behind that wall he put up between himself and others, women in particular. He'd denied the connection, the chemistry they had—hell, he'd even denied the friendship that had bloomed between them as he'd recognized she was as smart in her way as he was in his.

There were days when he just plain hated himself.

You can change, you know.

Why? His relationship with Sheryl had been no different. All Sheryl and he really had in common were sex and wedding plans. With Tessa it was sex and this case. That was nothing to base a relationship on.

All women are not created equal to Sheryl. If you don't give Tessa a chance, you might end up like that banana tree, all shriveled up and turning yellow.

"…meet you down there?"

"Sorry?" Griffin came out of his dark thoughts with a start, "What was that? I got distracted."

Petrie—what was her first name, anyway?—chuckled with understanding. "I said, how about I meet you down there afterward? The music doesn't start until nine. We can have a drink and compare notes. Say, around six?"

Down where? He'd completely lost track of the conversation. Didn't matter, anyway. He'd sooner talk to his banana tree. Better yet, he'd sooner go to a whole convention of psychics and talk to them.

"I'll give you a call when I'm done," he said. "I have your cell number."

"Good, that's a date." Then she paused a little self-consciously, the first human trait he'd detected in her. "I mean that in the time sense, not the social sense, of course."

"Of course." He said goodbye, disconnected and slipped the phone in his pocket. He'd make sure he was good and busy at six o'clock and conveniently forget to call.

His jacket hung on the coat tree by the door; the keys to the truck were on the coffee table. He grabbed both. He'd already told Jay he was going back to the beach house to search it. And now it seemed Tessa was confirming that was the right avenue to pursue.

His stomach rumbled and he realized he'd skipped lunch. Not that there was much in the house to eat, since he'd been at Jay's almost nonstop lately.

If Christina really was at the beach house, he was going to be eating a nice big helping of crow, anyway.

TESSA PULLED UP behind the beach house, set the Mustang's parking brake, and glanced at her watch. Wow. San Francisco to Santa Rita in an hour and twenty-eight minutes, not including the ten-minute stop at the In-N-Out for two cheeseburgers with no onion and extra pickles. Not bad for the old girl.

She got out of the car and followed the path around to the front of the house. It looked exactly as it had two days ago, except that this time there was a different air about it, a sense of life.

A sense of deeply unhappy life. Getting dumped was bad enough when you were a grown woman and at least had some tools with which to handle it. But getting dumped when you were still a teenager and only thought you were a woman was more painful still.

Tessa knocked and wasn't surprised when no one came to open it.

She tried the handle and, to her surprise, the door swung inward. *Christina,* she thought with a smile, *rule number one with secret hideaways is "Always lock the door."*

She stepped inside and closed it, noting that the red light glowed on the alarm keypad. Christina had even disabled that. Was she thinking that Trey would come back and wake her, like the prince coming for Sleeping Beauty?

Not gonna happen, girl. It would be more likely that some kid would walk in looking for a few portable electronic devices to sell at the flea market.

"Christina, it's Tessa. I'm a friend of your—of Mandy's. Can I come in?"

Silence.

"I know about Trey, sweetie."

"Get out of here," came a soggy voice from the bedroom.

"Your folks are worried about you."

She climbed the stairs and, from the end of the hall, saw a figure rolled in a blanket and curled up on the yellow bedspread. Tessa walked into the bedroom and put the bag containing the hamburgers on the table where Griffin had—

She pushed that thought out of her mind and unwrapped the first burger. After biting into it and savoring the fresh lettuce and tomato and making good and sure Christina could smell it, she pulled out the fries and squeezed ketchup on them.

"Getting dumped sucks the big one," she said, as though she and Christina had been buds for years and she was picking up a conversation where it had been interrupted. "What really sucks is building your life plan around the guy and then he treats it as though it's nothing."

From out of the folds of the blanket, two dark brown, suspicious, reddened eyes appeared. "What the hell do you know about it? Get out of here, bitch!" Then her angry gaze fell on the hamburger in Tessa's hand.

Tessa ignored the name-calling and popped a couple of fries in her mouth. "You probably haven't eaten since yesterday, right?"

Christina's hostile gaze tracked the fries from their cardboard container to Tessa's mouth.

"I got a burger for you, if you want it. Extra pickles, no onions." Tessa nudged the bag and smiled behind her burger as Christina threw back the blanket and scrambled across the bed. She grabbed the second burger and had devoured half of it before Tessa could maneuver the fries out of the bag. When that was gone, she offered Christina the other half of her burger, and when she'd eaten that, too, figured the girl's blood-sugar levels might be within human range once again.

"You owe me an apology for calling me a bitch," she said, and smiled. If Christina was anything like her dad, a firm stand was necessary right from the start.

"You're trespassing!" This was definitely Jay's daughter.

"Your dad hired me to find you. And I brought you supper. Two reasons why I'm not technically trespassing."

"My dad?" Christina frowned and poked a fry into the last of the ketchup as if she were stubbing out a cigarette. "Why should he care?"

"He cares. He's been a basketcase ever since you left. Tell me he isn't this cranky when he's normal."

The corners of Christina's lips twitched, then turned down again. "He's going to kill me."

Tessa shook her head. "He'll probably cry. I'm serious. It's clear to me he loves you like nobody's business, and I never met the guy before last week."

Could it have been just last week that her biggest problem had been deciding on a thesis topic?

"I've been working with Griffin Knox to find you."

"Griffin Knox? The security guy?"

"Yes. You see, I'm the one who got your blue cashmere sweatshirt."

"My what?" The girl looked completely lost.

"The ice-blue Stella McCartney sweater that you gave to some charity a while back for a fund-raiser."

Christina shrugged. "If you say so. What about it?"

Oh, to be so rich you didn't even know what one-of-a-kinds you were giving away.

"Well, I'm a sensitive. I learn things about people when I touch something they owned, like a watch or whatever. I got your sweater at a thrift shop and started learning stuff about you in a big way. So your dad hired me to see if I could help."

And I did. Even if no one believed me. Well, guess what, guys—I found her first.

"You found me from my sweater? Are you like a bloodhound or something?"

Tessa laughed. "No, it's more like I put on the sweater and a movie starts playing scenes from your life. Like when Trey bought those cotton scarves and tied you to the bed. Where was that, by the way?"

Christina's eyes widened. "You're bullshitting me."

Tessa shrugged and waited.

"That was here in Santa Rita. He wanted someplace anonymous so we got a hotel. Then I remembered Mandy's house from when she showed it to me once. She doesn't know I watched her punch in the code on the door."

And of course a girl brought up in houses that required expensive alarm systems would think nothing of remembering a key code.

"Have you had enough to eat?"

"Yeah. Thanks. I'm sorry I called you a bitch. You scared me."

"You shouldn't leave the front door open. He's not going to come back." Tessa tried to make her tone as sympathetic as possible. She was sympathetic. She had been in

Christina's shoes a time or two herself, dreaming the exact same fairy-tale dreams. Learning they rarely, if ever, had happy endings.

"The guy who really cares here is your dad."

Christina shrugged and dug her bare toes into the bedspread.

Tessa thought about the cards she'd thrown that first day, when she was trying to figure out what the visions of Christina meant. "Part of what I do is read tarot. You know, the cards?" Christina looked at her as though she were a lunatic. Tessa pushed on. "When I read them for you, they told me you wanted to start something new, that you had put yourself on a course and you meant to see it through. Is that true?"

"Yeah." Her tone was dismal. "So much for that."

"Well, what if it didn't mean Trey? What if it meant your relationship with your dad, or even getting into UC Santa Rita? I saw the applications in your room. You can do more with your life than give it to Trey Ludovic, Christina. The cards say you can plant the seeds and they'll grow."

Christina cocked an eyebrow at her. "Did anyone ever tell you you're weird?"

Tessa smiled, and nodded with wry acknowledgement. "Yeah, lots of times. But you know what? A lot more people tell me I'm right."

Except Griffin. The pain needled its way into her heart. She absolutely would not think about Griffin when there was a girl who needed someone to talk to right here. A girl who needed her family and a safe place while she recovered.

"So what do the cards say now?" Christina's tone was challenging.

Tessa reached for her purse. "It just so happens that I brought them with me." She took the velvet bag out and sat on the floor, her back against the footboard of the bed so that Christina could look over her shoulder and see the pattern the cards made on the rug. "I'm going to do a Hero's Journey spread for you. See, this is how it works. Kinda like *Star Wars,* you know, where Luke starts off in the Ordinary World…"

And that was how Griffin Knox found them when he arrived ten minutes later.

23

From the private journal of Jay Singleton

The saints be praised, it's enough to make a man go back to the Church. I never really believed in anything except myself, but this could almost convince me.

Christina is home.

She's well, unharmed, no bruises, scratches or anything else. I thought she'd be royally pissed that I had the cavalry out after her, but she seemed almost touched instead.

Ding-ding, Jay. Remember what Tessa told you. "She just needs to be with you," she said. "Needs to know that you appreciate her."

Okay, so maybe I'm the kind of guy who doesn't show it all that much. But Xena, who runs my office—I mean, Catherine, never seems to complain, especially when I give her another massive performance bonus. Mandy seems to be happy with the money and the sex. And redecorating rooms every time I walk out of them. But with kids it's different.

I only got to see Christina once a year after she was eight. It's hard to keep a relationship going, but I suppose I was hurt and figured Ocean Tech needed me more than she did. Despite my feelings about her mother, I can't deny she puts Christina first and does a fine job at parenting.

Is it too late to parent a young woman? Probably. But I don't think it's too late to learn to be a dad over again. If she's willing to let me fumble at it, I'm willing to try.

Jeez. Maybe I should quit writing it and just go tell her.

That's another thing Tessa said. "Say it out loud, Jay. She really doesn't know you love her."

For someone so young she's really wise. I don't know why Griffin isn't all over her like a dirty shirt. If I were his age and single, I might think about it, though I do wonder if she can read minds during sex. But he's acting like a bear fresh out of hibernation. Not that he was ever Mister Congeniality to start with.

I hear her voice in the hall.

Practice, Jay: *I love you, Christina.*

There. You can do it.

THE BONUS CHECK would pay the bills for the rest of the school year, with a little left over for a cap and gown. But that was less important to Tessa than the apology that came with it.

"I was wrong to have fired you," Jay Singleton said simply. Instead of sitting behind his massive desk like the corporate kingpin he was, he leaned on the front of it like a normal guy, with his ankles crossed and his shoulders relaxed. Even the volume of his voice was out of the red zone. Evidently having Christina back safe and sound was better than a dozen bottles of vitamin B.

"I know," she replied with a grin.

"Let me put that another way. I shouldn't have jumped to conclusions. What I should have done is followed the facts logically, the way I'd do with software code. Then I would have seen there was more than one interpretation when they weren't at the beach house the first time."

"Maybe." Tessa folded the check and tucked it in her handbag. "Or maybe what you should have done is trusted me. See how simple it can be?"

Jay smiled, and it wasn't a sarcastic smile, either. "There is that. So. What are your plans now?"

She shrugged. "Go home again, I guess. Pick a thesis topic. Be maid of honor at my sister's insane wedding. The usual."

"I have a feeling that life with you is never 'the usual.' If I ever need the services of a sensitive again, I know who to call."

"Thanks. I take referrals."

"And you can call me anytime. I mean that." Jay held out a buff-colored business card. "This is my private number, the one that doesn't route through the company phone system and my assistant doesn't answer. If you ever need anything—a job, a tow, whatever—you call me on that line."

"I don't suppose Human Resources would have much use for a psychology major at a computer company, would they?"

"Maybe not, but some days I need a shrink just for myself."

Laughing, Tessa wished him well and stepped out into the sunshine. There was no sign of Griffin anywhere—not that she'd expected him to be loitering around, asking for another chance. Not the King of Swords.

When he'd walked in on her and Christina at the beach house, she'd half expected a smile, a hug, some indication that he was happy about her success. But no. He'd merely asked Christina if she were all right and then called Jay on his cell phone. He hadn't asked Tessa why she hadn't done that in the first place, but she felt the question in the air as he'd placed the call and held her gaze while he'd ended Jay's misery.

So fine, she'd sacrificed the dad's peace of mind for the daughter's. On the whole, she felt she'd made the right choice, and Jay seemed pretty happy about the outcome if the check in her purse was any indication.

She'd parked the Mustang next to Griffin's truck when they'd brought Christina home. Pulling the keys out of her purse, she rounded the corner of the garage.

Griffin leaned on the Mustang's rear fender, looking as loose as a garage mechanic with nothing to do on a slow summer day. In her experience, though, garage mechanics never wore jeans that fit like that. Or had a body under them that was literally good enough to eat.

Tessa had a sudden visual of the last time they had made love and how he had tasted as he shuddered and came into her mouth. Her breath hitched and a pulse of desire darted through her belly to her groin.

Thoughts like this are not going to get you back to your normal life. Keep it low-key. Be cool.

"What's up?" she asked, tossing her purse in the passenger seat as casually as if the past two days had never happened. Or the past week, for that matter.

"Heading home?" he asked.

Some devil inside her goaded her to reply, "Well, if I were a detective I'd look at the resolved case and the car keys and come to the conclusion that yes, I am heading home."

If she had hoped for some kind of reaction, a nettled tone, a flash in the eyes, she was disappointed. He merely nodded. "How are you with plants?"

"Plants?" She stared at him, mystified.

"Yeah, you know, things that grow."

She tried to figure out why on earth it mattered now that she was never going to see him again. "Okay, I guess. I know about fertilizer and talking to them and stuff."

"Because I have this banana tree that's probably dying. I thought if you had nothing going on this afternoon you might come over and give me an opinion."

Banana tree. He wanted her to diagnose his banana tree. And men thought women were a mystery. Sheesh.

She wasn't quite finished with the King of Swords, anyway. She wanted to see him lower that blade. She wanted to hear "I was wrong not to believe you" coming out of those beautifully cut lips. She wanted to make him smile just once before she got back in the Mustang and left town in a cloud of dust, just like in the movies.

Okay, rewind.

She wanted to make him smile just once before he lost it and made love to her again. And for that she'd go and diagnose his banana tree.

"Okay," she said. "Lead on."

She followed him up the highway and into Santa Rita. He lived in a postwar community with houses painted terracotta and yellow and pale pink, with hibiscus and bougainvillea thriving in yards next to tricycles and the odd wheelchair. He slowed and pulled into the driveway of a house that was neatly kept, with a carved wood door that set off walls painted in a shade somewhere between cantaloupe and rust. Not what she would have picked for him, she thought, parking behind the pickup and switching off the engine. Maybe he'd bought it that way.

"Come on in." He unlocked the front door and stood aside to let her pass. The walls of the house were thick, allowing the interior to stay cool even when the temperatures nudged triple digits. The room was painted cream, and there were a few pictures of—were those chickens?—hanging on them. What the place needed, she thought, was a few of Mandy's bright cushions and striped slipcovers. This was the house of a man who furnished because he needed something to sit on, not because he needed something nice to look at while he spent time there.

Ooh, what she couldn't do with a house like this. Her student apartment was the house of a woman on hold, she realized. Everything was cheap, portable and fit easily in the back of a single truck, so she wouldn't inconvenience more than one friend when she needed a driver. The only things that said, "An individual lives here," were her plants.

Speaking of which...

"So, where's this poor tree?"

"In the back." He slid open the glass door behind the kitchen table. "Yesterday it was—" He stopped in the middle of the brick patio, gazing at something to the left. "Hey."

Tessa joined him, and looked in the same direction. "Griffin, there's nothing wrong with that tree that a little bit of water and some mulch wouldn't fix."

The tree was yellow around the edges and a little droopy, but other than that it looked pretty good. And here she'd been prepared to give it last rites.

"I gave it some of that yesterday. It must've liked it."

"When I was a kid my mom did a series of paintings of banana trees. Really sexual and over-the-top, you know? Big fruit and languid, serrated leaves in brilliant greens, reds and yellows. They sold like crazy. Anyway, she got a bunch of the trees in pots and it was my job to keep them alive in the studio until the series was done. I learned a lot that summer."

"About care and feeding of bananas?"

"No." She grinned at him. "About how sexy they can be. I was fourteen. What else do you think I was thinking about?"

THE SAME THING he and any boy his age had thought about when they were fourteen. The same thing he had forced himself not to think about between the time Sheryl had told him she was leaving and Tessa had come breezing into his life in her '66 Mustang and shot his beliefs about himself and his future all to hell.

Her gaze was still twinkling at him. "Come on, Griffin. You didn't ask me over here to doctor your banana. Or did you?"

Ninety percent of him had. The other ten percent—the part that craved the sight of that dimple in her right cheek and got tight in the chest over where the bows were tied on her blouse—would be delirious if she stayed to er, doctor his banana.

God, had he really asked her over here to do that? Could he get any more transparent?

"Look, I'm sorry," he said roughly. "That was pretty lame."

The sparkle drained out of her eyes like a slow leak. What had she been expecting? She'd driven away without a care in the world, just as Sheryl had, leaving him with nothing but pain and guilt. Even if it were self-inflicted in this case.

"Then what?" she asked.

There were so many reasons, not the least of which was that she was standing in the sun in those little pants that ended just below the knee, with two—he counted— thin knit tops with spaghetti straps in pink and lime green over that. He'd been trying to figure out for the last five minutes where her bra straps were. Maybe they were the skinny pale purple ones that—

"Griffin?"

Jeez. Could he for once focus on something besides her body when he was with her?

"I wanted to thank you, at least," she said. "For telling that detective to call me for information. That was nice of you."

"It wasn't nice at all," he said, his voice rough in his throat. "You send your investigator to the principal witness."

"She didn't believe me, but it still felt good. Like maybe you didn't think I was a fraud after all."

She was handing him his opportunity on a plate. "I don't think you're a fraud."

"Then why didn't you back me up in front of Jay?"

Ah, that was the question he'd been trying to answer all this time himself. He was silent for a moment, trying to arrange the words so they'd make some kind of sense. She bit her lip.

"Never mind." Chin up, she turned and walked into the house. "I can live without knowing."

"Tessa, wait."

In the kitchen, she faced him. "For what? For you to tell me you didn't really mean to humiliate me in public—again? Just because it turned out well doesn't mean it didn't happen. Or maybe you'd just like me to take care of your banana for you and get out of your life, like your other girlfriends?"

His mouth opened but no words came out.

"We had something special, Griffin, but as I told you before, until you quit pasting Sheryl's face on any woman who cares about you, you're just going to keep warding them off and being alone."

"I don't—" He cut himself off.

"Yes, you do. Then when they leave just like she did, you can tell yourself you were right after all not to get too close."

"The psychology major strikes again."

Brilliant comeback, Griffin. Guaranteed to make her stick around and go all warm and fuzzy on you.

"No, just a woman," Tessa retorted. "A woman who thought you might be able to drop that sword of yours and quit fighting long enough to get some joy out of life."

His sword? "What are you talking about?"

"That's your card, you know. The King of Swords. But if you're not careful you're just going to end up falling on it and living the rest of your life with a permanent injury. Is that what you want?"

The King of Swords. Now he'd heard everything. "You're not bad with a sword yourself. Are you having fun ripping me to pieces?"

His gut hurt, as if someone really had stuck something sharp under his heart. But was she doing it, or had he been doing it to himself all this time, and she'd just prodded a self-inflicted wound? Just how much pain could a man take before he realized something had to change or there would be no hope of healing?

"It's my job to tell the truth," she reminded him. "You should know that by now."

He did know it. And he'd come to depend on it, hadn't he, during their investigation. Why should he expect that she'd be any different now, when the case was over?

"The truth is a tough pill to swallow," he finally admitted.

"But isn't that what you spent your whole career looking for and trying to prove? So I bring it to you in a package that looks different. Maybe it has a few pieces missing. It's still the truth."

"So where does that leave us?"

She gazed at him, this woman who loved color and her car and the wind off the ocean. Who dealt in mysteries he couldn't understand the way he did with evidence and witnesses. Who lived with zest and perpetual optimism. Light to his darkness.

If he had to give that up again, he didn't think he'd survive.

He stepped across the gap that separated them and pressed her up against the counter where his coffeemaker stood, still without its carafe.

"Let me answer my own question," he said. "I believe in you. And you're right—I've been using Sheryl as an excuse to not get involved."

The sparkle was back, and so was the dimple. Giving in to temptation, he bent his head and kissed it, taking time to savor the softness of her skin. "And now?" she asked, a little breathlessly.

"And now the King of Swords wants to put the damn thing away."

"He can't retire it forever, you know," she told him, and wound her arms around his neck. "But he can ask the Queen of Wands to help him out. She has some practice at it, being royal and all."

"Is that what your card is?" he asked. "The Queen of Wands?"

She nodded, and her hair brushed his cheek. "I'm fire, you're air. I'm the body and the senses, you're the intellect. But we're both royal, both used to bearing our own burdens. A pretty good pair, really."

"And I suppose she's psychic, too," he teased.

"No, but she is confident about her abilities." She pressed her lips to the sensitive spot just below his ear. "And she's very, very sexy."

"Really." Goose bumps tiptoed down the side of his neck, and his body responded with a leap of enthusiasm. "Well, since I'm the intellect, you're going to need to prove that to me."

"Take me to the royal bedchamber and I will," she commanded, and the wattage of her smile warmed him right to his toes.

"That will be my pleasure," he said, and obeyed.

Epilogue

"THE NEXT TIME I say I'm getting married, just shoot me, all right?" Linn Nichols gave Tessa and Griffin a hug and sank onto the couch that Tessa was already plotting to have replaced. Linn looked around. "Hey, nice place. I see you're going to keep my sister in a style to which she'll become accustomed."

"Nice to see you, too." Griffin started a pot of coffee, placing the new carafe on the burner with what Tessa considered unnecessary care. "They treating you well at CLEU?"

Linn nodded. "The job is fine. Arresting importers is keeping me sane. Want to know what's happened now?" She glanced at Tessa in appeal.

"The store can't order our dresses."

"No."

"Kellan's mom can't do the flowers."

"No, she's fine. You should see their house. It looks like a florist convention."

"What, then?"

Linn paused for dramatic effect, then announced, "The parish hall where we'd booked the reception burned to the ground last night, and took part of the church with it."

"My God." Griffin sat on the edge of his recliner. "Was anyone hurt?"

"No, but they think it was arson. The sheriff's office is on it."

"Gosh. Maybe it was one of Kellan's ex-girlfriends, out for some revenge." Linn glared at her, and Tessa regretted the quip. This was not funny.

"Do you have any idea how long it took me to find that location? It never occurred to me to have my team do periodic surveillance on it on the off chance there would be arsonists."

"With two weeks to go, you're going to have to elope," Tessa said firmly. "I hear it's all the rage now."

Linn sighed. "I can't elope. I've already sent two hundred and fifty invitations. If you guys ever decide to get married, take your own advice and call me when it's over."

Tessa looked up to meet Griffin's warm gaze, and the corners of his eyes crinkled. They hadn't talked about anything as serious as marriage, much less eloping, but deep in her heart was the knowledge that Griffin was in this for the long term. And so was she.

The furniture, however, was not. Tessa gave the couch the evil eye. *Just wait. Your turn is coming.*

"So what we need to do is find you another place to have your wedding," Griffin said, turning his mind to his favorite leisure activity—problem solving.

"I've called everyone in three counties and unless I want to do it in the municipal park after the one o'clock Little League game, I'm out of luck."

An idea struck Tessa and she tingled, like the triangle does in an orchestra when it's tapped by a musician. "Are you opposed to doing it outside?"

"All the nice gardens are booked. That's why we went to Plan B, renting the parish hall."

Tessa stood up and went to find her purse. "I have an idea."

"An idea? What do you know about weddings? Tessa?"

She found her purse under Griffin's big bed, where she'd dropped it after being ambushed this afternoon and threatened with handcuffs until she agreed to make love for a solid hour. Still smiling at the memory, she retrieved her cell phone and punched in a number as she walked back into the living room.

Jay Singleton picked up his private line on the second ring.

"Tessa! Good to hear from you."

"And you. Say, is it true what I read in the paper? That Trey Ludovic is marrying that romance novelist who's worth a couple of million?"

Jay laughed. "It's true. She's ten years older than he is and about ten times smarter. The guy didn't have a chance. I don't have to tell you that Mandy introduced them at the Master's tournament at Pebble Beach."

"Mandy is the master."

"It took about a week, but Christina managed to get over it. She's starting at UC Santa Rita soon, so she has a lot to keep her mind occupied."

"I'm glad."

"So, what can I do for you? Is that Mustang of yours broken down on the highway? Need a lift?"

"No, we have a more serious breakdown." Swiftly, she told him about Linn, glancing at her sister as she did so. "So how would you feel about hosting the wedding of the century on your beach, with a reception on the lawn afterward? I know it's a lot to ask, but you wouldn't have to do a thing. The flowers and food are taken care of, and the band are all friends of ours, so they're portable. All we need is the real estate."

"Done," said Jay simply. "A week next Saturday, you said?"

"Yes."

"No problem. I'll tell Mandy right away. Let your sister know I'd be happy to have her and her wedding party as my guests the night before, too. God knows this house is big enough for an army."

"My gosh, Jay, that's awfully generous of—"

"Hey," he reminded her, "I've done this four times. I know how it is. Mandy will be delighted. It'll give her an excuse to zoom up to Neiman Marcus and buy a new dress."

"Jay, I take back all the bad things I ever said about you."

"Yeah, yeah, you and the *Wall Street Journal*. See you in two weeks."

"Take care of yourself."

"And you."

Tessa snapped her cell phone shut and beamed at Linn, who was looking as though a flash bomb had gone off in her face. "All set. A wedding on the beach, just like I always wanted. When you send the revised invitations, tell the two hundred and fifty people to wear comfortable shoes. Or maybe even none at all."

She crossed the room and parked herself on Griffin's good knee. He wrapped his arms around her while Linn struggled to speak.

"That was Jay Singleton," she said at last, as if corralling all the facts and pinning them down would help her take it in. "I'm going to have my wedding at his estate."

"Yup."

"Jeez, Tessa, what do you do for an encore?" Linn stared at her, her eyes lit with the dawning realization.

To-do lists were probably dancing like sugarplums in her head.

Griffin squeezed Tessa around the waist. "I don't know," he said in a tone laden with mock warning, "but the next time she plans a wedding, there had better not be two hundred and fifty people. Think about the security I'm going to have to come up with."

She looked deep into his eyes. "What next time? Is there something you're not telling me?"

He smiled at her. "You're the sensitive. You figure it out."

She closed her eyes in mock solemnity and cupped his face as though it were a crystal ball. "Hmm. I see sunlight in your future. I see a backyard with a banana tree that has miraculously come back to life. I see six or seven people and the mysterious absence of a ring bearer."

"Is that all you see?" Griffin asked softly.

She opened her eyes and gazed into the craggy, worn face she loved. "I threw the cards this morning, for real," she said.

"And what were they?"

"The King of Swords and the Queen of Wands. I think the universe wants me to know that the waiting is over."

"I could have told you that," he said, and pulled her closer for a kiss.

THE SECRET DIARY

**A new drama unfolds for six
of the state's wealthiest bachelors.**

This newest installment continues with

ROUND-THE-CLOCK
TEMPTATION
by Michelle Celmer

(Silhouette Desire, #1683)

When Nita Windcroft is assigned a bodyguard,
she's determined to refuse. She needs an
investigator, not a protector. But one look
at Connor Thorne—a quiet challenge begging
to be solved—and she realizes that having him
around all the time is a sensual opportunity
she can't resist!

*Available October 2005
at your favorite retail outlet.*

AMERICAN *Romance*®

40 & Fabulous

Dianne Castell

presents three very funny books about three women who have grown up together in Whistler's Bend, Montana. These friends are turning forty and are struggling to deal with it. But who said you can't be forty and fabulous?

A FABULOUS HUSBAND

(#1088, October 2005)

Dr. BJ Fairmont wants a baby, but being forty and single, her hopes for adoption are fading fast. Until Colonel Flynn MacIntire proposes that she nurse him back to active duty in exchange for a marriage certificate, that is. Is the town's fabulous bachelor really the answer to her prayers?

Also look for:

A FABULOUS WIFE

(#1077, August 2005)

A FABULOUS WEDDING

(#1095, December 2005)

Available wherever Harlequin books are sold.

Available this October from

DANGER BECOMES YOU

(Silhouette Desire #1682)

by Annette Broadrick

Another compelling story featuring

Brothers bound by blood
and the land they love.

Jase Crenshaw was desperate for
solitude, so imagine his shock when his
secluded mountain cabin was invaded
by a woman just as desperate—but only
Jase could provide help.

Available wherever Silhouette Books are sold.

HARLEQUIN®
Blaze™

COMING NEXT MONTH

#207 OPEN INVITATION? Karen Kendall
The Man-Handlers, Bk. 3

He's a little rough around the edges. In fact, Lilia London has no idea how to polish
Dan Granger. With only a few weeks to work, she has no time to indulge the steamy
attraction between them. But he's so sexy when he's persistent. Maybe she'll indulge...
just a little.

#208 FAKING IT Dorie Graham
Sexual Healing, Bk. 3

What kind of gift makes men sick? Erin McClellan doesn't have the family talent for
sexual healing. So she's sworn off guys...until she meets the tempting Jack Langston.
When he's still strong the next morning, she wants to hit those sheets one more time!

#209 PRIVATE RELATIONS Nancy Warren
Do Not Disturb

PR director Kit Prescott is throwing a Fantasy Weekend Contest to promote Hush—
Manhattan's hottest boutique hotel. The first winner is sexy, single—and her ex-fiancé,
Peter Garson! How can Kit entertain the man who's never stopped starring in all *her*
fantasies?

#210 TALKING ABOUT SEX... Vicki Lewis Thompson

Engineer Jess Harkins has always had a thing for Katie Peterson. He could even have
been her first lover...if he'd had the nerve to take her up on her offer. Now Katie's an
opinionated shock jock who obviously hasn't forgiven him, given the way she's killing his
latest project over the airwaves. So what can Jess do but teach her to put her mouth to
better use?

#211 CAN'T GET ENOUGH Sarah Mayberry

Being stuck in an elevator can do strange things to people. And Claire Marsden should
know. The hours she spent with archrival Jack Brook resulted in the hottest sex she's ever
had! She'd love to forget the whole thing...if only she didn't want to do it again.

#212 POSSESSION Tori Carrington
Dangerous Liaisons, Bk. 1

When FBI agent Akela Brooks returns home to New Orleans, she never expects to end up
as a hostage of Claude Lafitte, the accused Quarter killer—or to enjoy her captivity so
much. She immediately knows the sexy Cajun is innocent of murder. But for Akela, that
doesn't make him any less dangerous....

www.eHarlequin.com

HBCNM0905